India Yeti Pirates

Treasure Rebels, Volume 4

Gerard Doris

Published by Gerard Doris, 2023.

INDIA YETI PIRATES

First edition. September 25, 2023.

ISBN: 979-8223228349

Written by Gerard Doris.

Also by Gerard Doris

Treasure Rebels
Nile River Scorpion
Congo Spider Fangs
Amazon Swamp Victory
India Yeti Pirates
Greek Gladiator Sharks

Standalone
Wrath of the Renegades

Watch for more at https://www.adventurefictionforever.com.

Table of Contents

PROLOGUE: HIDDEN CAVE

(Bay of Bengal – India – One Month Ago)

The screeching bellow of a mighty Indian elephant echoed across the dark waters of the Bay of Bengal. The powerful creature stomped its immense feet in the mud along the riverbank, nervous and fearful. The forty year old beast refused to move away from the water's edge and instead continued to stare out into the dark gloomy night. Its owner, a young man in his early twenties ran up to the upset elephant and tried to calm it down. Soothingly he patted the creature's thick hide and spoke reassuringly, "It is alright Koby! It is alright!"

He paused and looked out at the quiet Bay. The surface of the dark water and the black night sky were impossible to tell apart due to the thick clouds blocking the moon and stars. The only thing visible were a handful of small lights coming from three immense container ships thirty miles away, each one headed out towards the Indian Ocean. Happily he took a long breath and enjoyed the peaceful moment until the lights finally disappeared from view. He then turned back to Koby and finally convinced his five ton friend to follow him back up the beach to where the other elephants and their owners were spending the evening and waiting for him.

"See my friend, there is nothing out there but the seagulls."

But the young man was wrong.

A couple miles away floating atop the smooth rolling waves was a small ship, every one of its on board lights eerily turned off. The only lights in fact were below the water, not above it.

Two faint lights twenty feet below the ship grew in intensity and size until they too were turned off.

Two scuba divers came out of the water like ninjas, both silent and invisible in the swirling shadows of mist across the Bay.

Dressed completely in jet black suits the two divers were carrying a large case, roughly the size of a large modern suitcase, and made out of bulletproof material. The two men silently kicked their fins until they were inches from the ship's blue hull. His face still completely hidden from view, one of the men whispered into a microphone inside his mask.

"Ready now."

Silently a rope ladder was dropped down from above until the bottom rung slapped the water's black surface. A second later an empty metal basket was lowered beside it. The divers carefully set the mysterious case inside, then as the basket was quickly pulled back up they climbed out of the water until they stood in the eerie darkness on the deck above. There was no-one to greet them.

They quickly took off their fins, tanks, and masks then hurriedly disappeared down a flight of aluminum stairs lit only by a few light bulbs that had been turned on seconds before. At the bottom was a very small cabin only half the size of a car garage. There were no portholes for anyone to see in from outside.

In the centre was an emaciated and intense looking Indian man in his sixties dressed in dilapidated sailor's clothes and nervously chewing tobacco. He was sitting by himself and studying the contents of the black case.

"You can turn the rest of the lights on now Dheeraj."

The old sailor tapped a cell phone in his skinny right hand and immediately the hold was filled with bright LED light from three fixtures in the ceiling. Dheeraj looked up from the case and grinned, every one of his fake white teeth reflecting the bright light.

"You got it Mr. Bombet! It is all here!"

He then jumped up and left the open case to shake hands with the youngest of the divers, a twenty-five year old Indian man with short cut black hair, warm brown eyes, and a very thin long scar that ran from his chin to just below his right ear. The scar suggested a violent past, but Darsh Bombet was no hoodlum, but in fact one of India's most proficient (and honest) treasure hunters. The thin scar had come a year before not from the pocketknife of a criminal but instead humorously from the sharp nail of a baboon that had scratched him during one of his expeditions into the Indian jungle.

Beside him Rhyce Tucker laughed and shook his head like a wild dog to rid his long hair of the saltwater from the dive.

"You're famous now mate! We'll be holding pirate treasure tomorrow!"

Pushing forty, born in New Zealand and already famous, Rhyce was a good friend of Darsh's and a tv celebrity. He specialized in creating travel documentaries with a focus on extreme climates and searching for archaeological treasures. While Darsh was humble and enjoyed the quiet hours of research needed to plan a treasure hunt, Rhyce preferred being in front of a camera and enjoying the fame that came after finding a treasure.

All three men quickly examined the open case. There were only three objects inside, each one covered in a velvet cloth. A ship's logbook sealed inside a glass case, a mysterious looking pirate axe pistol from the 1700's, and the preserved skull of a dangerous prehistoric creature.

A happy silence followed as they simply stared in awe, each man wondering how the world would react when the existence of the mysterious contents became public.

Darsh broke the silence and closed the case lid, snapping the locks back in place.

"Not safe yet. We can't relax till New Delhi." He then turned to Dheeraj.

"Is the speedboat ready?"

Dheeraj grinned back, his smile genuine despite the artificial teeth. "Yes Mr. Darsh! And fully loaded for the flight."

He then tapped his smartphone screen twice before raising it to his ear and speaking, "Take-off five minutes." Up above in the small wheelhouse his forty-something younger brother Arnav began to start the engines, and another series of lights came to life illuminating a passageway out of the small cabin.

"You two prepare in your cabins while me make your speedboat ready."

Two minutes later Darsh and Rhyce carefully stepped back onto the main deck wearing hiking gear and having left their scuba equipment behind. They shook Dheeraj's hand then climbed down into the speedboat where Arnav was storing two backpacks filled with supplies beside the bulletproof case. Arnav then climbed back up onto the wooden deck after which Darsh pulled the outboard motor to life and steered the small aluminum craft towards the muddy shore.

The weather had suddenly become a little colder and a light rain began to fall. Both treasure hunters shivered in the sombre weather, but neither man wasted a second worrying about the discomfort.

Darsh increased the throttle while Rhyce continuously scanned the dark Bay with night vision goggles. A half hour passed until the isolated beach materialized out of the cold rain. Rhyce tossed the goggles into the bottom of the boat and pounded his arm happily against the boat's side. "Triumph mate! Triumph!"

Darsh grinned but he didn't share the long haired adventurer's enthusiasm. His instincts told him it was too soon to relax.

As they approached the sand he killed the engine and took his eyes away from the shore for a second to look back. Just then sheet lightning flashed over the Bay and Darsh's heart skipped a beat as he saw what appeared to be three speedboats a mile away skimming the water's surface towards them. The lightning passed and the three objects disappeared again into the dark rain of the night.

"Grab the goggles!"

"What?"

"I think we have chasers!"

Rhyce tossed the rope aside and lifted the goggles back to his face. He studied the Bay for a full ten seconds.

"It's just some fishing trawlers mate! They've already stopped...they're casting their nets!"

He stuffed the goggles into his backpack then jumped out to secure the speedboat.

"It's all good mate! Triumph is still ours!"

Darsh instead waited, scanning the water for any sign or sound his friend was wrong. Nothing materialized out of the dark and the only sound was the splattering of the cold rain against the aluminum boat. Begrudgingly he turned away from the Bay for good and strapped on his own backpack, his eyes and ears having confirmed they were safe. But as he grasped the bullet proof case and stepped onto the wooden pier his sharp instincts still told him otherwise.

Putting on a brave face for Rhyce he slapped his friend on the shoulder.

"To the Pirate Cave!"

Rhyce laughed, his wild hair almost completely covering his face in the growing night wind.

"To the Pirate Cave!"

They walked out of the "beach" and reaching a small town hailed a taxi to drive them to a West Bengal train station. The driver was busy eating a late supper of butter chicken but was happy to toss the food aside for the large fare.

Over an hour later the taxi pulled into the station and Darsh and Rhyce stepped onto the dimly lit platform to wait. Nervously Darsh watched the fifty other men and women also waiting to board. Five minutes later the old but sturdy train flew into the station on time. They hurriedly boarded and took seats opposite one another. The overhead lights in the narrow car skipped a moment then came back to full power as the train lurched forward and pulled away from the bright lights of the town and sped into the dark countryside.

Darsh watched the platform disappear into the night and finally began to believe that Rhyce had been right all along. There just couldn't be anyone following them.

Three more hours passed quietly, except for two peddlers who wandered through the cars trying to sell books, water, newspapers, and sandwiches. Hoping to finally be left alone the two treasure hunters gave in, Rhyce buying a two day old sandwich while Darsh bought the last copy of a daily newspaper. The elderly peddlers thanked them and politely left, eager to find new customers in the forward cars.

Rhyce tossed the sandwich out the window into the darkness and instead lit a cigarette grinning impishly.

"I love the Indian rail system mate...they let ya smoke!"

"Not anymore."

Rhyce angrily snuffed the cigarette out just before a security official could be seen entering their car. "Right mate. Health and safety and all that nonsense."

Darsh turned back to the window and his mind drifted wondering how his life would change once their discovery became public. Movie deal? Book tour? Those were the things Rhyce wanted. What he wanted was for the world to know the Yeti Pirates were real.

He turned back to the newspaper which seemed to contain nothing but cricket and field hockey scores, weather predictions, interviews with politicians, and ads for Bollywood. He reached the last page and realized it was just another ad for an upcoming film, depicting an incredibly beautiful red head trekking through the jungle with the headline: LOST IN THE AMAZON RAINFOREST.

He sat up in his seat and realized it was no movie ad but a real life news article. And the woman was none other than Amber Monette, one of the world famous Treasure Rebels. He furiously scanned the article which stated that she and fellow treasure hunter Travis Jagson were diligently searching the Amazon to find the renowned Maddox Tarver who had disappeared days before. He finished reading and wondered whether the leader of the Treasure Rebels would ever be found. He then pushed the thought out of his mind and settled in for what would be an agonizing long journey.

Fifteen more hours later the sturdy train hissed to a stop for the last time, having covered almost fifteen hundred kilometres. They were now in New Delhi, India's capitol and home to over twenty million people.

Impatiently they were amongst the first passengers off the train. They quickly spotted a taxi and Rhyce handed the Sikh driver a very generous amount of Rupees and directions. The driver happily grabbed the money and sped through a handful of narrow streets narrowly avoiding parked scooters and the occasional sad looking stray dog, the windshield wipers working to clear off the afternoon rain. Thirty minutes later the taxi rolled to a stop at a small airplane hangar on the outskirts of the city.

They knocked on the old office door until the manager with tired bloodshot eyes let them in. He handed them a series of papers to sign then led them to a small room where a table covered in food had been laid out, with two chairs and a small flat screen tv.

"Everything is as you ordered, yes Mr. Bombet?"

"Everything looks fine. We leave at midnight."

"Midnight it is."

When the clock finally hit twelve a.m. they jumped up and followed the manager outside where a white twin engine private plane sat fuelled and ready for take-off. They were ready to see the Himalayas.

"We've modified it to carry extra fuel as you ordered."

The manager then handed Darsh a rare looking key.

"Your special car will be waiting for you at the base of the mountains sir."

Rhyce laughed as they jogged towards Darsh's plane.

"488 GTB?"

"F12 Berlinetta. It was a gift from my father."

In minutes they were airborne, Rhyce in the pilot's seat with Darsh in the co-pilot's chair studying the mysterious contents of the black case. He carefully lifted the axe pistol and pulled the flintlock safety back. It still worked. He replaced the safety then examined the curved edge of the axe blade then the large and pointed emerald green jewel at the base of the handle.

"The axe edge is gone. But the rest of the pistol looks strong."

Rhyce looked at the nasty looking axe blade and grinned.

"But just think what it could still do if chopped into bone!"

Satisfied at the overall quality of the axe pistol Darsh returned the old weapon to the safety of the case and with a loud *snap* he locked the lid before closing his eyes for a two hour rest.

They each took turns flying and in nine hours the mighty tops of the Himalaya Mountains could be seen in the far distance sticking through the clouds and early morning mist.

The white plane slowly descended until it coasted over a small road then dropped another couple hundred feet until the wheels touched the grass of an empty field below a gravel roadway. Rhyce cut all the power while Darsh lifted the two backpacks and the black steel case out of the back. Darsh then carefully pulled out a small revolver from a cabinet between the back seats. He snapped it open and looked inside. Unsatisfied with what he saw, he snapped the gun back together and left it in the plane.

Rhyce locked the plane doors then tossed the keys to Darsh who threw the tv personality his backpack. Together they then jogged towards a grove of nearby trees.

Barely visible beneath a thicket of tree limbs and brambles were fifteen containers filled with gas to be used for the return flight, and the edges of a dull grey tarp. Together they each grabbed a side and with a snap of their wrists the tarp and branches pulled away...to reveal a beautiful red Ferrari F12 Berlinetta. They quickly loaded their backpacks and the metal case into the surprisingly large cargo compartment in the back then jumped inside. Darsh inserted the key then hit the red start button on the bottom of the wheel and the 731 horsepower engine came to life.

He hit the accelerator pedal and drove the car up the grassy hill and onto the dilapidated road. But once the wheels left the grass he kept the mph speed low. With a rough road surface and a forty foot drop on each side, he didn't want to risk a spin out or tear up the wheels.

Then he saw the two dirt splattered pickup trucks eerily following behind. It was not suspicious to see trucks on the road at this early hour, but whenever Darsh slowed down or sped up the two dirty pickups did the same.

"Rhyce! We aren't alone!"

His friend looked back puzzled then stuck his head out the passenger window to get a better look. With his long hair flying in all directions he studied the two trucks then leaned back into the car just as the road wound to the right around a giant boulder. Darsh quickly took the curve to see the road ahead suddenly dip fifty feet then straighten out for the next half mile on smoother tarmac in a large valley.

"Waste them."

Darsh pushed the pedal and the Ferrari accelerated, reaching the end of the valley in a matter of seconds and beginning the climb up the other side. He then tensely looked back through the rear-view mirror. The two trucks hadn't even reached the curve around the boulder yet.

Rhyce slapped the arm rest and chuckled.

"See? They're just farmers carryin' rice or vegetables. We're in the clear mate!"

They reached the top of the valley and continued on, the pickup trucks disappearing behind them for good.

The next thirty minutes went smoothly with only a handful of old vehicles passing them in the opposite lane. Finally Darsh sighed in relief as he turned the wheel and the Ferrari spun off the main road and up a small dirt lane that was almost hidden from view. In two minutes the dirt path twisted left then right a dozen times as the red supercar wound through the stony hillside. Rhyce was instantly lost but Darsh knew every turn.

"We're almost there."

The path suddenly ended before a stone wall that stretched high into the pale blue sky. There was nowhere to drive and the face of the black stones was obscured by a thin sheet of water falling from the top of the hillside almost a hundred feet above.

"You didn't tell me about the waterfall part!"

Darsh's grin finally returned as he switched on the Ferrari's high beams and slowly drove forward.

"Welcome to the pirate cave!"

The supercar quietly rolled forward into the water until the lights revealed a dirt path. To Rhyce's amazement he realized the waterfall was nothing more than a natural cover for the cave's entrance.

Darsh tapped the controls and the wipers cleared the windshield. Carefully he pressed the accelerator down ever so slightly and stared forward in awe as the front lights lit up the cave's shadowy interior.

The cave was roughly twenty feet high and had been naturally carved out of brownish silt and stone, with smooth floors of natural stone partially covered in sand and black dirt. The lights stretched forward for hundreds of feet but no end could be seen. It looked more like the beginning of a large tunnel than a simple cave entrance.

"Hit the wipers!"

Darsh looked up to see a small strangely coloured snake slithering across the windshield. He tapped the controls and the windshield wipers swept the poisonous creature away into the shadows.

They drove slowly forward. There was nothing to see but light dust swirling in the headlights and the occasional Indian Krait snake, also extremely venomous, stuck to the cave walls. After another minute the walls became covered in snakes, most of them oddly coloured and impossible to identify.

"I thought the pirates were exaggerating when they said the cave was *full* of serpents."

Darsh waited to respond, instead watching with growing fear as the headlights illuminated a bright green snake almost ten feet long and curled around and slowly eating what looked to be a large rat.

"Or how big they get."

Darsh avoided the unusually large Bamboo Pit Viper then followed the tunnel around a tight bend which led into the centre of a much larger cave. Ten times as wide as the tunnel, the cave's ceiling was also a hundred feet high above the car, covered in a light frosting of cold dew which had begun to turn into ice. High above three large goats stuck their heads through an opening in the ceiling and watched the red Ferrari below. Then tentatively they climbed down into the cave, standing atop a narrow crevice which protruded from the stone wall. But after seeing two Russell Vipers slither towards them they immediately climbed back into the sunlight and disappeared from view.

Down in the dirt below Darsh cautiously drove the supercar around a half dozen Himalayan Pit Vipers slithering near the wheels. Once past the snakes he ignored a handful of tunnel openings to his left, instead driving into the farthest tunnel to the right.

This tunnel was even smaller than the first and only spacious enough to fit a large SUV. But the sand and grime were gone, now replaced with a natural cold stone floor, and the Ferrari's wheels now gripped the "road" more tightly.

After another minute of driving the small tunnel slightly expanded to roughly ten feet in height and width. In seconds the headlights revealed the end of the tunnel a hundred yards ahead...completely covered in strange looking wood. Darsh put the Ferrari in park twenty feet from the obstruction but left the car running. Together they each then grabbed new sledge hammers from behind the two seats and slowly approached.

Rhyce paused and slowly patted the old timber, slightly stunned.

"Can't believe it...*real* wood from a *real* freakin' pirate ship."

Darsh grinned and readied himself while lifting the sledge hammer to strike.

"Forget that! I want to see the *real* pirate treasure!"

Rhyce laughed then together they began to break the wooden barricade apart with powerful strikes. The decaying wood splintered, cracked, and easily broke away, and in moments they were back inside the supercar and driving into the darkened insides of the pirate cave system.

What the lights revealed was the largest tunnel they had seen yet, with a stone wall to the right of the vehicle and an eerier precipice to the left. The ceiling was over two hundred feet above.

"How close is the treasure?"

Darsh pointed into the distance beyond the current reach of the lights.

"The treasure den should be at the end."

He drove forward smoothly to avoid the dark precipice, each rotation of the wheels seemingly bringing them closer to mythical pirate gold.

But he suddenly groaned in frustration and slowed to a crawl because of what the headlights revealed through the gloom up ahead.

Fifty feet away a large tree stump lay directly in front of them. Darsh looked for a way around but with the precipice to their left and the stone wall to their right there was nowhere to go. He was forced to put the car in park thirty feet away from the barrier.

"No worries Darsh!" Rhyce grabbed one of the sledge hammers then opened his door and stepped out. "It'll be rotted and break apart easy!"

Then the tree stump moved.

Rhyce dropped the sledge hammer and leaped back into the car slamming the door in an almost hysterical panic.

"Back up! You know what that was!"

Darsh frantically put the car in reverse...to see the back lights reveal the pathway behind was now suddenly blocked by another dark shape.

"It must have circled behind us!"

Darsh didn't hesitate, shifting gears in a heartbeat. He smashed the pedal down and the Ferrari shot forward. For a half dozen seconds the tunnel wall flew past on their right and the only thing that could be heard was the roar from the Italian supercar's engine bouncing off the cave walls.

Until the faint yet eerie sound of a large animal hissing pierced through the engine noise...and then the back end of the Ferrari rattled violently as something in the dark smashed brutally into it...and Darsh lost control.

The car spun sideways then finally flipped and stayed overturned, sliding across the smooth stones while pieces of metal and glass flew in all directions. The car finally stopped and an unnerving quiet filled the ancient rocky tunnel, made much worse by the lack of light thanks to the front headlights now having been shattered to pieces.

Twenty feet away Rhyce slowly climbed to his feet, his hair covered in glass and his right arm covered in wet blood. If he had a mirror and a flashlight he would have seen the top half of his left ear was missing. He ignored any pain he felt and almost laughed when he realized he had been tossed clear of the car and astonishingly somehow survived. He then hobbled to the overturned vehicle and looked inside.

Darsh was still sitting in the front seat, groaning in pain and covered in glass and black dirt. But Rhyce saw no blood, or any sign of his friend being pinned inside.

"Darsh!"

Darsh coughed in pain, but then a second later he nodded his head okay.

Rhyce stood back up and grasped the door handle. But before he could open it the car lurched forward as something smashed viciously into the passenger side, and Rhyce was thrown to the side while the Ferrari tumbled towards the precipice. Rhyce screamed in terror as the supercar and his friend inside disappeared over the edge and he could hear the car hit the bottom in the darkness below.

Complete silence greeted Rhyce as he painfully stood and stumbled in the dark towards the edge to look down. Then suddenly the quiet was broken and he heard again the frightening hiss louder than ever coming from below the precipice where the Ferrari had disappeared.

Rhyce hesitated and thought of searching in the dark for the sledge hammer to protect himself, and then climbing down into the dark and using it to smash a car window if needed to get Darsh out.

But the hissing suddenly intensified as the creature drew close and Rhyce decided what he would do.

He turned and desperately ran.

Choosing instead to leave behind a trail of blood, the supercar, his friend, and a shocking creature no living person had seen before.

PART I: THE FAVOUR

(New Delhi – Present Day – Train Station)

The passenger train slowly rolled into the dilapidated station, the heavy rattling and screeching of the coach's wheels echoing across the crowd filled platform. The train stopped, the whistle blew twice to signal arrival, and the passenger car doors were opened with a loud crack.

Travis Jagson and Amber Monette were the first to step onto the platform. Ten feet away an underweight bald man wearing a silk business suit waved at them. He was holding a sign with the carefully printed words: TREASURE REBELS.

The sign wasn't needed because no one else on the platform looked like the two treasure hunters.

At six foot five inches and two hundred fifty pounds, Travis Jagson was one of the strongest men on earth. Built like a weightlifter the thirty year old from Hawaii had given up his professional boxing career when asked by the famous Maddox Tarver to instead become a treasure hunter. He never hesitated at accepting the offer, and roughly two years later he was now one of the world's most famous experts on archaeology and underwater excavation.

With her natural red hair Amber Monette was even easier to spot amidst the crowd. She was stunningly beautiful and her bright turquoise eyes reflected her high IQ, but more importantly her happy carefree soul. When Maddox had promised her he would recover a little known medicine to save her father from a rare disease, she immediately left her career in astrophysics and agreed to become a member of the team. Eventually Maddox fulfilled his promise by finding the medicine in the jungle of the Congo.

But what the Treasure Rebels as a team had been chasing for over two years continued to elude them.

The self-conscious man in the business suit quickly lowered the sign and rushed across the platform to greet them. Shaking their hands he then led them through the crowd of hundreds to a waiting Mercedes limo in the parking lot. With a huge smile he opened the car's back door and motioned them to step inside.

"My employer Mr. Nihar Bombet is extremely excited to see you again! You may call me Jalaj. We will go now to his estate!"

They climbed inside to see champagne, two flat screen tv's, imported cigars, and freshly cooked lamb waiting for them in the spacious backseat. Travis ignored most of it, instead opening a bottle of water resting in a bucket of ice and turning one of the tv's to an American sports channel. Amber simply laid her head back and began reading from her specialized tablet.

Nihar's happy employee climbed into the driver's seat and the black Mercedes slowly pulled away into the late morning traffic. The minutes ticked by as Jalaj drove through a series of heavily crowded streets filled with scooters, walking pedestrians, green coloured three wheelers and old signs hanging above the pavement.

Travis finished the water and slowly picked up one of the cigars and then the lighter hesitantly.

Without turning away from the tablet Amber said, "You already know what I think."

He shook his head, putting the lighter back onto the silver tray but pocketing the cigar for later.

Still not looking up she quickly put on a pair of ear buds attached to the tablet, then watched and listened intensely as a video message was played. Three minutes later she tapped the screen and pulled the buds off.

"Your Dad?"

"He's already through analyzing Wolfgang's notebook, and now he's testing the treasure dive helmet. He expects a breakthrough any hour."

The tablet beeped and a blue digital box appeared in the screen's upper corner.

"Another video message?"

"No, he just sent me a hundred pages of theories as to what Wolfgang's old journal notes could mean. Rather confusing stuff. Even with all of the papers from the Congo safe to help us, my father still can't understand half of the notebook's contradictions."

"Maddox will make sense of it."

The Mercedes left behind the dilapidated buildings and crowded streets and pulled into a newer section of the city and a much broader side street that bordered a busy highway. Jalaj quickly spun the wheel and turned the Mercedes into a quiet red pebbled courtyard with a large bubbling fountain in the centre. Circling the large fountain were eight luxury supercars, including the Bugatti Chiron Amber and Travis had last seen in Brazil. Barely visible through the grove of trees a small private runway and landing pad for helicopters could be seen off to the side as part of the mansion grounds.

Jalaj pulled the limo up to the curling white marble steps and put the car in park. Still smiling he then led them up the steps and opened the twin eight foot high mahogany doors.

"Follow me to the study."

They followed him up a gold plated staircase and through the first doorway at the top of the stairs.

"Mr. Bombet will visit you in moments! Enjoy his collection while you wait!"

With that he stepped back out into the hallway and disappeared back down the stairs.

The study was immense; the cherry wood floor was covered in plush gold coloured carpets while the walls were paneled in old dark wood. Apart from an open walking space in the centre, every wall and corner was filled with exotic artefacts, preserved animal fossils, timeworn paintings, and old military weapons resting in display cases or pinned to the wall. Near the door was Nihar's eight foot long wood desk, which looked as if it had been built during the Middle Ages. The only modern objects in the entire room were the plush leather chair and super car key stand behind the desk, and a top of the line computer with a 40 inch monitor placed on top of it. Despite a large window which overlooked the courtyard and fountain below, most of the room was still poorly lit giving the study an almost eerie feel.

Surrounded by thousands of years of history they quickly split up.

Travis passed a hundred year old painting of the Himalayas, then paused in front of a glass case with the words *Napoleonic Wars* carefully written above. In the case was a broken short Saber from a Russian Grenadier and a bearskin hat and nasty looking axe both stained with blood that had been used by a French Sapper. Sitting on a glass plate beneath the bearskin was a set of French handcuffs from the early 1800's which had been used during the wars.

The next case beside it was twice as large, containing the rotted frame and smashed wheels of an Egyptian war chariot and a well preserved Khopesh (sickle sword). Above the glass case was another painting depicting the Egyptians engaged in brutal warfare in the desert against an unnamed enemy. The oil painting was in near perfect condition and not surprisingly featured a war chariot in the centre of the fight, carrying two archers who had just killed three foot soldiers who lay crumpled lifeless under the chariots wheels and horse's hooves.

"Travis! Look at this!"

He walked back to find her pointing at another glass case, surprised disbelief written across her face. He looked inside and said, "It's just a large dinosaur footprint."

"Read the description!"

He bent down and read the small plaque out loud: *"Discovered in the 1890's by a local farmer, found inside a cave near the base of the Himalayan Mountains."* Travis looked closely at the stone footprint which was three times the size of a human being, clearly able to see the claws at the end of the five toes. Amber pulled her tablet out of her knapsack and said disbelievingly, "It looks like a cross between a human and bear!"

"He better not tell us a Yeti kidnapped his son."

"Do not worry Treasure Rebels. I do not believe in Yetis!"

They turned to see Nihar Bombet enter the study carrying a DVD and smartphone while smiling at their interest in the exotic footprint. He was dressed much the same as he had been in South America, except now he also sported thick rimmed glasses. Also, despite his cheery mood the stress he was under had turned his goatee even grayer than when they had seen him only a week before on the beach in Brazil.

"May I take a couple photos?"

Nihar waved his hand in agreement as he sat down behind the thousand year old desk. "By all means go ahead Miss Monette!"

She lifted the tablet and took five photos of the odd footprint made out of stone and the metal plaque beneath it.

"Thank You!"

Nihar nodded his head and placed the DVD into the computer tray and closed it.

"How is Mr. Tarver?"

"More banged up than we expected. He wants to thank you-"

Nihar cut her off as the DVD began to play on his 40 inch screen.

"No thanks are necessary! I'm just glad the Treasure Rebels have decided to help me!"

He then stared intensely at the large screen for ten seconds with a pained expression on his face, before turning away and typing out a long text message on his silver black phone. As Amber turned back to continue studying the strange footprint, Travis instead continued watching Nihar with a slight sense of unease.

Despite everything the rich man from India had done for them, Travis still couldn't shake how he felt. Nihar annoyed him. A lot. He felt guilty at disliking the man who had saved his friend and he couldn't figure out why the feeling never went away. He guessed it had something to do with Nihar's slightly eccentric personality. But in the end he decided it didn't matter. What did matter was that Nihar had found Maddox, and he was going to return the favour and find Darsh.

The smartphone suddenly chimed twice and Nihar looked up pleased.

"He will be here any second."

Amber and Travis looked at each other with surprise. "Who?"

Before Nihar could respond Rhyce entered the study. Along most of his right arm was a hideous looking scar from the car crash and his left ear was bandaged from recent plastic surgery.

"This is Rhyce Tucker, a friend of my son's. He was with Darsh when the car went missing."

Rhyce looked at the two Treasure Rebels with a questioning smirk across his face.

"Where's spiky hair?"

Amber hesitated before replying, "Maddox will be meeting with us later."

Travis just stared back cooly at the reality tv star.

Nihar then quickly turned the monitor around so the others could see the flat screen. Images of the mountain road, cave entrance, Ferrari, and of Darsh played across the screen. "Tell them the details."

Using the images on the screen as prompts Rhyce explained Darsh's disappearance by beginning with the night dive in the Bay of Bengal, the train and plane rides, and the Ferrari drive to the caves. He then continued, "We entered the cave to find it filled with snakes, some nasty big and poisonous. Deadlier I'm sure than the kind you three have seen in the jungles. There were so many we were afraid they were goin' to crawl right inside the car. Then, well..."

He took a deep breath, and the stupid grin finally left his face as the story became grim.

"The Ferrari hit a large animal. Actually flipped it over." He then lifted his arm, the sunlight revealing in greater detail the nasty fleshy wound. "I was thrown from the car, Darsh was trapped inside. I tried to help him but the car disappeared down a large ditch of some kind. I couldn't get back to the plane on foot, so Darsh's father here picked me up near the cave. We've tried to rescue Darsh twice since, but we can't get past those gallin' snakes which have nearly tripled in number."

Nihar added indignantly, "I contacted the police numerous times. They half-heartedly searched, claiming it was too dangerous to travel far into the cave tunnels. An outrageous claim! I even offered them ten million rupees but they still refused!"

Nihar stopped the DVD then continued, "We have assembled a team of men to help in the search. The very best equipment, and we've even obtained full medical supplies which include a collection of anti-venom shots for various snakebites."

Amber grimaced as she asked the obvious question. "I don't mean to sound uncaring Mr. Bombet, but the odds of your son being alive after all these weeks is close to impossible. We don't want you to get your hopes up."

Nihar smiled and placed the DVD back in its case grinning broadly. "My hopes are well grounded Miss Monette! Listen to this!" He tapped a few keys on the keyboard then hit the Enter button. Instantly the faint sounds of a cell phone recording began to play. The audio quality was poor, but they could clearly hear pieces of the brief message through the static, *"Dad I'm okay. I'm trapped in the car...Food running out...Tell Rhyce to hurry back! Please!"*

Nihar hit the Stop button. "His battery must have run out because the message ended there."

He then looked up from the desk with a new found look of determination. "But I heard that message only two days ago. He lives! I know it. And you Treasure Rebels are the ones to rescue him!"

Rhyce then turned to leave, "We'll take the plane in twenty minutes. After landing we'll take the SUV's up the mountain road to the cave." He then pointed for everyone to follow him out. "Everything's ready!"

"We're not ready."

Nihar and Rhyce looked up in disbelief as Travis pointed back at the computer screen.

"Why the Ferrari?"

Rhyce replied puzzled, "Why?"

"Why would your buddy Darsh drive a supercar into the caves? Professional treasure hunters would choose something really tough like a specialized Hummer. He's lucky he didn't rip the car's guts out on that mountain road."

Nihar shrugged his shoulders and waved towards the window overlooking the fountain and cars outside. "My son shares my love of the fast super car. He always *insisted* on driving fast. He took the Ferrari from me before I could talk sense into him."

Amber then fired off another question.

"Why did you and Darsh dive in the Bay at night during bad weather? You both broke about a dozen safety and common sense rules doing that."

Rhyce smirked mischievously, "We could taste the treasure...we couldn't wait. Every good treasure hunter knows that feeling can't be ignored."

"You mean every dead treasure hunter."

Rhyce looked away to Travis hoping for an easier question. Instead he got another tough one.

"Why did you and Darsh spend the entire night rushing across India to get to the mountains? Other treasure hunters after the pirate loot?"

Rhyce genuinely froze for a split second then answered, "Darsh was human like the rest of us, you know? Honourable guy, but human. The closer we got to the treasure the more nervous he became. Convinced crooks in the black market were watching us, hoping to steal the treasure and sell it illegally. It was his plan to race to the mountains the moment we retrieved the artefacts. I never agreed with him, never saw anyone *ever* who looked suspicious. But I let him draw up the plans because he was the one financing everything mate."

Travis folded his immense biceps across his chest and asked further, "Seen any signs of activity near the cave since the crash?

"None. No new tracks of any person or vehicle."

Amber asked the final question, "Is it possible the Ferrari was ambushed by people in the cave and not some animal?"

"Naw it was an animal. I could hear it hissing, and a putrid appalling smell."

"Did you get a good look at it? Maybe the car's back wheels hit an oversized Water Monitor Lizard causing Darsh to lose control?"

"Couldn't see much in the dark."

He then abruptly turned to Nihar, "I better double check to see if we're ready to fly. See you all on the tarmac out back in twenty."

Nihar agreed then excitedly stood and pointed towards the far end of the study which was mostly hidden by shadows. "Before we leave for the plane I must explain what my wonderful son was looking for in the mountains!"

They followed him through a series of display stands and statues until he stopped in front of something unlike anything else in the entire room. Before them was an immense glass case almost ten feet high and fifteen feet long. The interior was in darkness until Nihar tapped his smartphone's screen. Instantly a dozen small lights embedded in the top of the display case flashed on. What they revealed was incredible.

Resting beneath the bright lights were five dummies wearing 18th century naval uniforms Travis and Amber had never seen before. Nihar waved his hand and announced, "Pirates unlike any other!"

Each uniform was a mixture of sailor's tunics and breeches, with military style belts and sashes to carry pistols and sword scabbards. Lining each pant leg were also straps to carry exotic daggers into battle. Each pirate also wore a large overcoat whose hoods were lined with wolf fur, while the outside of the overcoats were protected by a thick layer of brownish white fur from an unidentified animal.

Sitting on hooks were a series of pirate pistols, Indian bandaq matchlock muskets, and oddly shaped swords that resembled a scimitar but were smaller and more sinister looking. These "scimitars" were coated in silver and the sword hilts were engraved in an unknown language. Beneath each blade was a plaque with the inscribed words: *Yeti Slasher*.

Silence filled the room for a good five seconds until Travis turned to Nihar.

"You lied. You do believe in Yeti's."

"No! No! I certainly do not!"

He then turned back to the display case and continued, "These sailors were called Yeti Pirates and considered almost a myth even in the days they prowled the Indian Ocean. Except for a handful of documents and these recovered uniforms and weapons it would be impossible to prove they existed."

"Who found all this?"

Nihar smiled proudly, "My son found everything you see here! As you know he is great treasure hunter and explorer, though not as famous as you Treasure Rebels."

Nihar then lifted the smartphone and pointed it towards the blackened wall above the case while tapping the screen once again. "And this was his greatest discovery!"

Instantly the wall was illuminated by another series of small lights, revealing the largest oil painting in the study. It depicted the interior of a massive Himalayan cave, where the pirates wearing the same uniforms sitting in the glass case were shooting and fighting with a large creature over ten feet tall and covered in brown white fur. The beast was howling and was holding one of the pirates in its left claw, while at its feet lay two more pirates covered in blood with their necks clearly broken.

Nihar quickly explained, "Please ignore the Yeti in the painting! After the pirates quit robbing ships they became what you Westerners would call...big game hunters. A written account from a merchant in China shows he was paying them incredible wealth to bring him the hides of exotic animals. My son believes as I do that the pirates stored their hides and money in a Himalayan cave, and fearing that others would try to find their treasure hoard, they had this artwork created to spread the false rumour of a terrible Yeti living in the cave. To complete the illusion, they spread myths of Yeti sightings that never occurred and claimed to be the only men on earth who could successfully track and kill a Yeti."

He then pointed to the Yeti footprint near his desk and continued, "You've already examined one of their better illusions! The "footprint" is nothing more than a primitive form of plaster and stone. But for reasons unknown, after 1740 there are no further records of the pirates. My son thinks they died in a mighty hurricane that same year, and therefore their treasure still waits to be recovered in the cave!"

He then smiled even more broadly.

"And after you find my son he will assuredly allow you to follow him into that very cave when he discovers the Yeti Pirates wonderful treasure!"

The two Treasure Rebels looked at one another, knowing what the other was thinking. They turned back to Nihar and Travis explained, "We're just interested in finding Darsh. We need to be back home as soon as possible."

Suddenly Rhyce reappeared at the front of the study, the self-satisfied smirk having returned. He quickly nodded his head that their ride was ready.

Nihar quickly tapped the smartphone and the pirate artefacts and painting were again shrouded in darkness. "Let us now go to your famous friend!"

==

(The Next Day)

Nihar's three modified and reinforced V8 Hummers pulled to a stop on a hill near the base of the Himalayan Mountains.

As Travis, Amber, and Rhyce exited one of the vehicles, five hundred feet above a green helicopter slowly flew down towards them, coming to a rest on the frost covered grass three hundred feet away. Before the rotor blades had even come to a stop Travis and Amber began walking towards the helo while the side door slid open and the lone passenger hopped onto the ground. Amber hugged the man while Travis shook his hand and happily slapped him on the shoulder.

Maddox Tarver was back.

With his spiky blond hair, distinctive sunglasses, and confident wild smile the twenty-something famous leader of the Treasure Rebels looked the same as he always did, except for the sling his left arm was now in. Together all three Treasure Rebels walked back to the vehicles where Rhyce and two of Nihar's men were waiting. Fifty feet away Nihar leaned outside the passenger window and waved to Maddox before disappearing back inside his own vehicle.

Rhyce shook Maddox's hand and pointed at the copper coloured sunglasses that hid Maddox's eyes.

"Cool shades. I never thought I'd meet the world's most famous treasure hunter."

Maddox smiled, "You're the one on tv man."

A brief moment passed as the "reality" tv star and the man who actually lived the reality sized each other up.

"Nihar told me about your injuries. Shoulder going to be a problem?"

"Just a broken bone and separated shoulder. Almost healed."

The arrogant smugness disappeared from Rhyce's face as he listened to Maddox and responded, "I've been a friend of Darsh's for over ten years. You coming here, broken shoulder and all, I want to sincerely thank you." He then shook Maddox's hand before nodding to Nihar's men it was time to go.

In moments the small convoy resumed its journey towards the mountains while the green helicopter took off and flew in the opposite direction. In twenty minutes the vehicles climbed a small hill before turning onto the very road the Ferrari had taken about a month before.

Rhyce looked back from the front passenger seat to the Rebels who were sitting in the back.

"Won't be long folks!"

He then paused for a second before speaking directly to Travis.

"I was there in Miami four years ago...you know, that amusing night you won the heavyweight belt by knocking out-"

"I remember."

"What's more fun...lifting treasure out of the sea or lifting that belt over your shoulder?"

Travis hesitated, uncomfortable at the comparison.

"I love what I'm doing now. Simple."

Rhyce nodded his head slowly. "Obviously. The big money alone you three have found makes it clear you were smart to quit that boxing gig."

Irritated, Travis looked out the window at the Himalayan countryside as thoughts of his sister still lying in a hospital bed in a coma filled his mind.

"Nothin' to do with money."

Rhyce didn't hear Travis and instead turned to the others.

"What do you think of Nihar's ride? Everything is top of the line. Every switch and feature!"

He then pointed to the dashboard which contained an unusually large number of buttons.

"He had extra equipment installed in case we need it, winches, top of the line CB Radio, extra gasoline tank, and even a secondary airbag system which can be activated after the first set has been used!"

Rhyce paused for effect but when he didn't get the expected surprised looks from the Treasure Rebels he gave up and hurriedly announced, "We'll be there in minutes."

The convoy reached the thin waterfall and with the Treasure Rebels in the lead car they left the open road behind and entered the cave. The walls were crawling with snakes and Rhyce confirmed that there were now three times as many serpents as when he and Darsh had visited before.

The minutes slowly ticked by until they reached the large cave with the multiple tunnels. Once again a handful of wild goats could be seen peering down from above while their hooves clung to the same outcropping of stone near the ceiling. Rhyce directed the driver to head towards the tunnel exit on the far right, the headlights revealing hundreds of strange coloured snakes moving along the walls.

In the last vehicle Nihar peered out at the snakes, pulling at his goatee nervously. He then looked back at the medical kit in the SUV's trunk and turned to the driver.

"Do you recognize any of these snakes?"

"Just the Himalayan Pit Vipers on the ground. The ones on the wall I've never seen before. Good chance they're a newly discovered species."

"Do you believe they're poisonous?"

"If they're venomous it's hard to say whether the anti-venom in the back would help or hurt."

Nihar sighed. "Then no one opens a door or window without my say."

"Understood sir."

Boom!

Just as the man finished speaking the windshield *smashed* inward as one of the large goats crashed into the glass from above! The driver hit the brakes and the stunned animal dropped onto the ground. Unbelievably the wild goat stumbled to its feet still alive, and in a panic immediately jumped up and began climbing the stone filled wall before the snakes could catch it.

Visibility was now impossible. But that wasn't Nihar's biggest problem. A slim ten inch purple snake quietly slithered into the SUV through the now porous glass, slithering across the dashboard and finally wrapping itself around the gear shift near Nihar's left hand.

The moment Nihar noticed the snake it was already too late to react. He lurched back in fear but the snake's fangs were faster. With a howl Nihar felt the bite.

The driver reached across and grabbed the creature, opened his door and roughly tossed the small snake into the dirt. He then snapped a photo of the serpent with his smartphone in case the snake needed to be identified later by a doctor. Finally slamming the door shut he looked at his employer.

Nihar's face had turned frighteningly white and his hand was dripping red blood. Despite the small fangs the snake had bitten deep.

Nihar simply nodded his head and the driver knew what he had to do. He grabbed the CB Radio and called for the helicopter that had dropped Maddox off to pick them up. He then quickly radioed the others, explaining what had happened and that he was taking Nihar to the hospital as fast as possible. When Rhyce grabbed the mike and spat back they would follow, Nihar took the mike from the driver and ordered Rhyce and the others to continue, "Go ahead without me! My son needs each of you! Another delay could mean his death. I will report back to you as soon as I have news. Do not worry about me. Good luck Rhyce. Good luck Treasure Rebels!"

The driver leaned forward and pushed the windshield completely out, then spun the Hummer to head in the opposite direction. As the Treasure Rebels watched, Nihar lifted his arm through the window and waved goodbye to them, his face full of alarm that his last day on earth may have arrived.

As Nihar's vehicle disappeared from view a nervous silence filled the air. The Rebels looked at one another stunned but still determined.

"He's right. We can't help him but we can still help Darsh."

Rhyce agreed with Amber then after speaking with the other vehicle's driver the remaining two Hummers continued forward into the small tunnel. They reached the end without incident then drove through the splintered remains of the wooden pirate door Darsh and Rhyce had broken through with the sledgehammers.

A heavy blackness enveloped the remaining two SUV's as they drove deeper into the cave. Each vehicle's headlights revealing nothing but large stones lining the pathway and the dim outline of the Ferrari's tire tracks in the brown chalky dust. Finally the tracks ended where the Ferrari had flipped over.

"Stop here." Maddox ordered.

The Treasure Rebels along with Rhyce stepped into the dark carrying flashlights. Travis and Amber cautiously walked to the edge of the pathway and shone their lights down into the large trench. Maddox instead stayed where the crash had occurred and bent down on one knee to examine the tire tracks. With his back to Rhyce he ran some of the dirt through his fingers, a look of nervous reflection filling his sharp eyes behind the sunglasses.

"Did the creature bite the car?"

Rhyce looked down and froze.

In Maddox's hand was a thin serrated tooth, oddly curved and roughly half the length of a pencil. Rhyce remained speechless until Amber's voice cut the silence.

"We see the car!"

Maddox put the tooth in a leg pouch and joined his friends along with Rhyce at the pathway's edge. Sure enough, thirty feet down the luxury car's silver exhaust pipes and back wheels could be seen in the light off to the right. Rhyce quickly lifted the walkie-talkie to his face and gave the order for the Hummer's to pull up.

As the vehicles drove forward Maddox turned to Amber and handed her the exotic tooth.

"What we're up against."

She nodded and placed it on the tablet screen, typing a quick command on the screen keyboard. Instantly the display turned red as a gold line began traveling across the screen beneath the tooth, similar in look to the way a photocopier scans a page. The tablet gave a quiet beep and she handed the eerie tooth back to him.

"I'll let you know once the tablet has a match."

For the next few minutes the Rebels along with Rhyce lowered climbing ropes over the precipice while securing the lines to the bumpers of the two remaining Hummers. Next the Rebels pulled out one of their own specialized equipment bags. Inside were tranquilizer guns, extra ammunition clips containing tipped darts, sharp Bowie knives, flashlights, canteens of water, and sleek ultra-modern night vision goggles. The night vision lenses did not protrude like a pair of binoculars but instead more closely resembled the tinted lenses worn by snowboarders and mountaineers, except larger and with exotic rims.

Maddox calmly pulled off the sling and tossed it into the Hummer. He still felt a little pain but he simply couldn't climb unless his shoulder was free to move. Then certain Rhyce and his team weren't watching he slipped the sunglasses off and clipped them to a jacket pocket before sliding the night vision mask over his eyes. He then tapped a small ON button atop the frame and the lenses suddenly glowed a bluish red in the dark.

Now fully ready for the climb down the Rebels left the rest of their equipment (including their specialized chainsaws) in the Hummers for now. Rhyce approached the precipice carrying a fully loaded hunting rifle. He threw the weapon behind his back and sharply called back to Nihar's four men as he tapped the radio strapped to his shirt.

"You see anything up here you let me know pronto. And if Nihar rings patch him right through."

"Of course." He saluted them then pulled an older and bulkier night vision helmet over his long hair.

They stepped to the black edge as Maddox took the lead.

"All ready?"

Amber looked at the tablet screen as the built in sensors beeped twice. Air quality was good.

"Ready!"

Together the Treasure Rebels and Rhyce began the climb down into the dark towards the trapped Ferrari and Darsh.

As they descended each climber would pause every few seconds to turn and scan the trench...just to be sure they were still alone and no animal was waiting for them at the bottom.

All clear so far.

In two minutes their boots touched the cold stone of the trench floor and they slowly approached the wreckage.

Rhyce and Amber each called out Darsh's name but no response came. Amber then lifted the tablet as if it were a camera and typed a command. The tablet beeped again and a strange bluish image filled the screen. Growing worried she turned to the others.

"No signs of body heat. Hope it's just the debris blocking the reading."

They slowly walked closer uneasy what they would find beneath the rubble. They quickly began lifting and throwing the boulders and smaller stones away until the car's windows were completely visible, calling out Darsh's name every few seconds. No response.

With trepidation they shone their lights inside the cockpit. Dozens of bottles of water, empty cans of processed food, and the black case lay on the empty passenger seat...but no Darsh.

They swung their lights across the dashboard to reveal the windshield was completely missing, and that beyond the Ferrari's front hood was not a stone wall, but the opening to another smaller passageway. It was clear that the Ferrari had been pushed up against the new tunnel's opening, where the stones had then sealed it in place. It appeared Darsh had given up waiting for help and had crawled through deeper into the caves.

"Goin' in!"

"Maddox wait!"

He didn't wait and climbed inside. He then lifted the bulletproof black case out to Rhyce who gratefully took it.

The tv personality mumbled a thank you and stepped back as Travis and Amber followed Maddox. He then leaned inside the Ferrari and looked through the empty space where the windshield had been and at the Treasure Rebels who were now waiting in the small passageway for him.

"I'm going to send this back up for the boys to keep. It's too heavy for me to carry. You three go ahead and I'll catch up."

Maddox was already ten feet ahead of the others but he abruptly stopped.

"No man. We need to stay together as one. We aren't goin' forward without you."

Rhyce nodded his head in understanding. "Smart. I'll be right back."

Impatiently the Rebels watched as Rhyce disappeared and all they could hear were his steps as he walked back towards the climbing ropes outside in the trench.

With nothing else to do they studied the mysterious passageway which appeared to have been naturally made and was roughly eight feet wide by ten feet high. Their night vision lenses pierced the darkness for fifty feet to reveal nothing except the faint outline of Darsh's boot prints and a large brown coloured scorpion slowly crawling across the dirt.

Travis quietly pulled out the tranquilizer handgun and took aim. But before he could fire the poisonous arachnid had reached the other side and disappeared through a small crevice.

Amber turned her head and looked back at the empty interior of the Ferrari.

"We should have told Rhyce to bring back an anti-venom container. Could be hundreds of those things or more snakes down here."

They waited another minute for Rhyce to return. Nothing.

Travis finally had enough and stepped out of the small passageway and back into the car. He then leaned his head out the window and called for Rhyce to hurry up. Nothing.

He then quickly climbed out of the car still calling out to Rhyce and scanning the open trench in every direction. Nothing.

He then looked up to the edge above but no one was visible. But he did hear the engine booms of the Hummers and he immediately ran in the direction of the ropes. Behind him Maddox and Amber were now climbing out of the car. They all knew something was wrong.

He reached the rendezvous spot then stared at the stone wall in angry silence. The climbing ropes were gone.

High above the two Hummers sped away and vanished in the direction of the pirate cave. He furiously spat on the ground as his friends joined him, the sound of the vehicles still echoing off the walls.

"He just betrayed us and Nihar. That wimpy traitor is gon-"

He was cut off by the sound of Amber's tablet beeping. She lifted her arm and pulled the tablet off her velcroed sleeve. Even in the dim light they could see from her expression it was something terrible.

"The tooth?"

She nodded to Maddox and explained.

"According to this the tooth you found doesn't belong to any known reptile or mammal."

Travis scowled, "Not a Yeti match!"

She shook her head and tapped the screen to keep scrolling as she read the text.

"No...but it does come close to matching a real creature...that's supposed to be extinct."

Maddox and Travis looked at one another as she concluded, "Guys, it looks like it belongs to a relative of the...Titanoboa dinosaur snake."

Just then the sound of the Hummer's engines in the tunnel above finally faded...and was replaced by the horrid sound of hissing.

PART II: DARSH

They looked up where the chilling sound came from and their night vision masks picked up the rapid moving image of a large snake slithering along the edge of the tunnel above them...a snake with a body as wide as that of a tree trunk. The large black body suddenly swivelled and the creature's head became visible, five times larger than a modern Anaconda and filled with teeth that glowed green in the darkness of the cave...and then it began to move down the stone wall towards them.

"Run for the Ferrari!"

They reached the car in a matter of seconds, the sound of the hissing growing in strength as the immense snake drew closer with every second.

Amber dove in headfirst and was already crawling past the broken windshield into the small passageway when she was followed by Maddox. He ignored the pain in his shoulder and with both arms slid into the supercar in one motion. A second away Travis reached the car but turned and unloaded two tranquilizer shots at the monstrous snake, stunned at the speed at which the creature moved. Both darts hit the snake directly in the head...and bounced off harmlessly.

Travis jumped inside and rolled onto the car's dashboard. Maddox and Amber reached through where the windshield had been and pulled him forward into the small passageway just as the snake smashed headfirst into the supercar's back fender. The car wobbled violently and the Rebels turned and continued to run the moment they saw the green teeth enter the car's cockpit.

After ten seconds two large scorpions crawled into view twenty feet ahead. Each arachnid stopped and turned to face the oncoming Rebels, taking threatening positions and raising their strange multi-coloured tails and poisonous black stingers.

Maddox and Travis simply took aim and fired. The darts hit with enough power that both arachnids were blown off their feet, rolling in the dirt until they came to a stop, unmoving except for their eight legs which twitched involuntarily.

They stepped past the scorpions then ran forward a hundred feet. Then another hundred until they were forced to stop at the eerie sight before them.

Dozens of glossy dark coloured Indian Krait and brown Russell Vipers blocked the way forward, slithering and curling through the dirt. Most were snapping at one another as they fought over territory, while the stones of the passageway's ceiling and walls were covered with smaller unidentified snakes slithering away to avoid the serpent brawl in the dirt below.

The Rebels looked back. They couldn't see the Ferrari from this distance but it didn't matter. They could hear the hissing intensify in the shadows. The gigantic snake with the glowing teeth had gotten inside the passageway.

Trapped between a man eating snake the length of a bus and a horde of deadly serpents, it was a time when most would freeze in horror.

Maddox instead just grinned and double checked the ammo in the gun, "Man, I'd rather die of poison than getting eaten."

Travis and Amber grabbed their own tranquilizer pistols and couldn't help but grimly smile at Maddox's bravado. All three then nodded to one another and ran forward towards the poisonous Kraits and Vipers. They fired at the snakes relentlessly and each serpent that was hit with a single dart crumpled into the dirt paralyzed. But there were too many snakes to shoot and they were forced to run *through* the mass of serpents that were still awake...and venomously angry.

Maddox ran ten steps forward, his boots only touching cold stone, dirt, and the limp bodies of two drugged Vipers. He kept shooting and when the trigger finally clicked empty he jumped forward head first over the last few snakes and rolled onto the empty ground to safety.

Travis took a different approach. He fired repeatedly at the snakes lining one of the walls then leaped for clear ground beneath the same spot. The second his boots hit the dirt he then stepped up onto an outcropping of stone now free of any serpents then jumped over the rest of the venomous creatures below. Two Vipers leaped upwards to strike him but both sets of fangs impacted harmlessly into the reinforced soles of Travis' boots. He was in the clear.

Amber followed closely behind her friends easily stepping around the serpents. She neared the end and seeing Travis roll to safety she prepared to jump...but with three feet to go a Russell Viper unexpectedly curled its body directly into her path. She stepped onto the snake's head and tripped, dropping into the dirt which was filled with the unmoving bodies of paralyzed snakes.

Before she could jump back to her feet two oversized dark bluish Kraits curled onto her back, wrapping themselves around her neck and shoulders.

"Don't move!"

She froze amidst the bodies of the paralyzed snakes, paralyzed herself through fear.

One of the Kraits stopped moving on her right shoulder, and twisting its body back paused with its black eyes and quivering tongue only a half foot away from her face. It then paused as if waiting for Amber to move before striking. Things only got worse as the other serpent slithered onto her left shoulder before gliding into her red hair stopping at the top of her crown, hissing in agitation the whole time.

Out of ammo Maddox and Travis watched in horror. The only option was their blades and slowly standing they slid the Bowie knives out of their leg holsters. Carefully moving forward they approached the two snakes from different sides. But they were forced to stop as each uneasy step only made the serpents even more distressed.

But suddenly both Kraits stopped hissing and their threatening postures immediately changed. In a split second they turned away from Amber and slid back onto the ground where they then slithered towards small crevices amongst the stones lining the passageway wall. They weren't the only ones, as every snake in the small passageway was hastily moving towards the wall to seek a way out. The reason was obvious.

The monstrous snake with the glowing teeth was getting close.

Travis and Maddox reached down and pulled Amber to her feet in one motion, and together they ran in the opposite direction. The path abruptly changed and they were forced to run steeply uphill. A long minute later the passageway finally flattened out once again before it twisted into a curve twenty feet away.

They paused to give their stinging lungs a chance to recover, while Amber's face was still pale white from her experience with the snakes. They looked downhill behind them but the night vision lenses revealed no sign of the enormous snake.

They rested another ten seconds until Maddox nodded his head and they continued forward. They reached the curve which coiled sharply right for thirty feet, and exiting it they stopped in shock.

Darsh.

Lying in the dirt his face hidden from view, the young adventurer lay still, his clothes covered in grime while a blood stain on his vest was visible beneath the shoulder blades.

"Snake venom got him."

"We don't know that Travis!"

She knelt down beside Darsh and examined him, taking off her night vision mask and instead using an LED flashlight which provided better light up close. She suspected Travis was right but wasn't giving up hope.

She discovered he had a strong pulse and was breathing steadily, so she carefully poured water on his face. It worked and he jolted alert, coughing violently and struggling terribly to sit up.

He had lost twenty pounds of weight, had a thin beard, and his forehead and black hair were covered in dust while a streak of fresh blood ran across his face. His clothes were torn and there were nasty blotches of dried blood near his left knee and right arm. He was lucky he could still walk.

He looked up at Amber with a look of absolute shock, believing he must be hallucinating.

"You're...you're from the newspaper. You are famous woman. You can't be real."

She handed him another canteen relieved he was alert enough to speak.

"I'm very real. I'm Amber Monette."

He continued looking at her slightly dumbfounded before turning the canteen upside down and drinking until it was empty. Off to the side Travis and Maddox continued to watch for any sign of the dinosaur sized snake.

The adventurer from India handed the now empty canteen back and with Amber and Maddox's help he slowly stood, his physical and mental strength returning. With joyous relief he shook their hands thanking them over and over.

Amber then asked, "How did you get past the snakes?"

Darsh coughed brutally then explained, "Not too hard. Only four of five snakes in here. Just avoided them. Did you see them too?"

"Four or five dozen."

He thought she was joking and began to laugh a little but stopped and instead coughed even more fiercely, leaving behind a streak of blood and grime from his lungs on his sleeve.

"Did you find Rhyce Tucker? He is a friend of mine and was with me when the car flipped-"

Travis shook his head and interrupted.

"He ain't your friend...or ours."

"What? That is-"

"The minute we located your black case he took off and left us to die. We saw him last drivin' deeper into the caves looking for your pirate treasure, with a Hummer full of Vultures who work for him."

Darsh shook his head sternly and objected. "No! Rhyce has been my best friend for over a year! These men must have kidnapped him or threatened him or..." He searched for words and was visible angry, but the hesitation and look in his eyes revealed his own doubts of Rhyce's loyalty.

Amber handed him another canteen of water and a spare flashlight, "You know these mountain caves much better than us. Can you lead the way out?"

He opened the canteen and replied, "Yes, and once outside I can lead us to my plane. Rhyce and I hid it along the roadway." He then looked at her puzzled, "But don't you want to find the treasure first?"

"No, we're just repaying a favour to your father."

He didn't seem to listen to her response, instead he poured a third of the canteen over his head and blinked, the freezing water bringing him to life even more. He then stood and took three uneven steps before anxiously looking at the three of them.

"We must go back to where the main tunnel is! That is only way I know which leads out."

As Travis and Amber hurriedly blocked his path and began to explain the Titanoboa like creature, Maddox moved past them in the opposite direction, his intense eyes scanning the rocks.

"Hear that?"

They stopped talking and paused, expecting to hear the dinosaur hiss coming from the gloomy passageway behind them.

Instead Maddox grinned and pointed forward.

"Rhyce's Hummers."

=======================================

A minute later they stepped clear of the tunnel to see before them another giant cave containing a forty foot wide pathway which was lined on one side by a giant wall which extended over four hundred feet up to the ceiling. On the left side of the stone pathway was an empty abyss. While the first large cave had a thirty foot drop into a trench below, the drop off for this precipice was straight down over a hundred feet into the dark bowels of the cave system.

Only twenty feet below them the two reddish black Hummers were idling in the pathway, the exhaust from their tailpipes visible in the chilled air.

Maddox and Travis both took off their night vision masks as well to instead rely on their own LED flashlights for the climb down.

"Let's say hello to Rhyce."

Darsh nodded his head and was about to reply to Maddox but stopped, surprised at the ugliness of the twisted damaged tissue he could briefly see around Maddox's eye sockets. Instead he simply followed all three Rebels as they carefully climbed down the twenty foot embankment. Reaching the end they turned off their lights to avoid being spotted then quietly stepped onto the reinforced metal of the first SUV roof. Very slowly Travis peered down and looked through the small back window into the cargo compartment. Empty. He correctly guessed the rest of their equipment was instead stored in the lead vehicle. They would have to leave it all behind.

He lifted his head and nodded to the others. Amber turned to Darsh who was nervously holding onto the roof as if he was on a terrifying ride at an amusement park, even though the large vehicles were still stationary.

Once she had gotten his attention she pointed behind the Hummers into the darkness and spoke quietly, "See? We just have to follow this path back to the main tunnel. Get ready to climb down when we tell you."

He apprehensively nodded his head but before they could make a move the dull clink of the Hummer's gears being changed reached their ears, followed by the sound of the tires chewing over stones and dirt. The Hummers were moving again.

The seconds went by and it became clear that Rhyce and his criminal friends intended on driving forward carefully. As a result the Hummers went no faster than twenty miles per hour. Darsh closed his eyes and pressed his face against the roof as he held on. The Rebels instead prepared to jump clear while they still could.

Amber leaned forward and shook his shoulder. "We have to jump Darsh...now! Before they speed up."

He slowly lifted his head, his face full of alarm. But it had nothing to do with the thought of jumping.

"That sound!"

The Rebels looked at one another for a second puzzled until Maddox understood.

Uneasily he looked up the embankment at the tunnel from where they had come.

Slithering down the stones at an unbelievable speed was the monstrous creature, its glowing teeth and tongue growing brighter the closer it traveled towards the Hummers.

Now visible in the dim light of the Hummer's back lights, the Rebels could see the prehistoric looking reptile was about forty feet long, and while most of its scales were black they occasionally glimpsed the underbelly which was a pale yellow. The snake's body was about three feet wide and there were two large sets of fins behind the head. Unlike a cobra's hood, these flaps looked more like the wings of a manta ray, and they opened and closed as the creature moved, giving the appearance it was almost flying across the ground.

They also could see it was traveling twice the speed of the two Hummers.

Instinctively they jumped forward onto the roof of the first vehicle.

Rhyce looked up from the front passenger seat at the sound and barked at the driver.

"What was that?"

The man paid him no attention and was instead looking at the side-view mirror which reflected the image of the forty foot snake closing in. "Rhyce...look!!"

As the men inside both cars now started yelling in a panic, the Rebels quickly secured themselves to the roof of the lead Hummer as best they could. Travis grabbed Darsh's shoulder and spoke directly to the weary Indian treasure hunter, "Hold on buddy, every bit of muscle you got!" Almost collapsing with fatigue Darsh weakly nodded his head then clung to the roof with all the strength he had left...a second before both vehicles accelerated in a furious frenzy.

The snake increased speed as well, its winding body covering the passageway at an incredible pace. But as frightening as the reptilian creature was, it became clear that it was no match for the Hummer's V8 engines. After ten nervous seconds the glowing teeth began to fade behind a cloud of dust in the rear view mirrors.

Then everything got worse as a new pair of glowing jaws emerged into view through the headlights.

Another colossal snake was fast approaching in the opposite direction *towards* the lead Hummer. It had the exact same colour and glowing fangs as the monstrous snake that was chasing them from behind...except for one difference.

This serpent was even bigger.

The driver screamed at Rhyce in rage, "I thought you said there was only *one monster*!"

His eyes bulging with terror Rhyce didn't even hear the driver as he watched the oncoming snake which was now only a hundred feet away from the windshield and closing fast.

The driver continued steering *towards* the creature, timing the moment perfectly when he swerved around the massive snake's head, the glowing teeth missing the windshield by inches. Above Darsh lost his grip and the young adventurer began to fly sideways off the SUV roof...until Travis reached out and grabbed him with one arm and pulled him back to safety. Darsh clung to the steel railing once again, too terrified to yell in agony because Travis had accidentally pulled his already damaged shoulder out of its socket.

The enormous creature spun in the dirt to give chase, blocking the entire road directly in front of the oncoming Hummer from behind. The second SUV crashed into the snake's curled body, flipping onto its side and sliding towards the cliff edge...where it tipped over and spun end over end until four seconds later it struck the boulders far below and detonated on impact. The three men inside were immediately incinerated by the explosion.

High above the largest snake gave up on the lead Hummer carrying the Treasure Rebels and Darsh and instead curled over the edge and slithered down towards the smoking ruins of the destroyed car far below. The "smaller" snake continued forward to try and catch the remaining vehicle.

The SUV accelerated at an incredible speed and in seconds the glowing teeth began to disappear behind the churning cloud of dirt and engine exhaust once again. But then the flat surface of the pathway unexpectedly became uneven and filled with severe bumps and ridges. The Hummer was going too fast for the driver to adjust in time, and the back half of the vehicle lifted off the ground for a second as the front end slammed into a series of deep potholes. The driver was forced to use the brakes to prevent a spin out while the Rebels and Darsh were nearly thrown onto the front windshield.

The Hummer jolted back and forth through the dirt ridges and protruding stones for another two seconds...then the pathway became smooth once again. But it was too late.

The forty foot serpent appeared out of the dust until its head was parallel with the Hummer's right side door, then with a loud hiss it swung its head and glowing teeth directly into the passenger window shattering it and lifting the Hummer up into the air.

The Hummer landed with a crash but continued forward leaving pieces of the back fender and a million shards of glass flying behind. Somehow everyone atop the roof held on. The creature lost twenty feet in pursuit but quickly gained speed and curled to attack the vehicle from the opposite side.

Inside Rhyce was almost shrieking in fright covered in glass while he saw the snake close in again. Hands anxiously shaking he grabbed a black machine gun off one of the back seats. He then leaned out the front passenger window to shoot...

Only to have Travis reach down and happily rip the gun out of his hands!

"Thanks buddy!"

Travis then sat up, aimed the Uzi at the creature's hideous face as it drew close to the car's back wheels, and pulled the smooth trigger.

A wild streak of reddish orange flame shot out of the muzzle as every sizzling bullet cut through the chilled mountain air. Each round hit the frightening creature but the monstrous snake only slowed until it was ten feet behind. It never stopped gliding forward. Travis let go of the trigger and repositioned himself for the second blast.

"*Travis*!"

He looked down at Amber who was pointing forwards.

"*Hold on*!"

He turned his head to look and realized the ride was about to get a lot tougher.

The smooth stone road ahead was about to become little more than a patch of uneven dirt ridges once again.

The SUV flew into the heavy dirt, the tires instantly losing traction in the soft almost sand-like surface. In seconds their mph dropped from fifty to twenty while the back wheels flung streaks of dirt high into the air as the Hummer slid from side to side.

As the vehicle slowed the snake drew close to strike and swerved again to the right side of the vehicle, the bullets from the machine gun having only scarred the reptile's thick outer scales on its hideous face and body.

"Grab my legs!"

Barely holding onto the roof themselves, Amber and Maddox leaned forward and held Travis' legs to the roof. The monstrous reptile suddenly lifted its head until its eyes were level with the Treasure Rebels and Darsh, and with another freakish hiss it opened its jaws allowing a stream of green black saliva to slap across the passenger back window.

This was it.

Travis leaned out over the edge into empty space, twisted his body to face the oncoming snake, and unleashed thirty bullets directly into the creature's open reddish jaws.

Pieces of the snake's teeth flew in every direction as the bullets tore into the reptile's unprotected flesh and in pain it immediately turned its head away from the sliding SUV. Curling away it dropped behind the vehicle and slithered into the dust filled distance, leaving behind a thin trail of blood and a half dozen teeth embedded in the Hummer door...each one still glowing green.

Travis pulled himself back up to the others his face dripping with sweat but smiling like a winning championship fighter.

"Good thing ol' Trav—"

The snake reappeared on the other side of the Hummer and without hesitation it swung its head savagely into the vehicle just above the back wheel, crushing part of the Hummer's outer plating and lifting the SUV into the air where it crashed onto its side and began to slide in the soft dirt towards the cliff edge.

The Treasure Rebels and Darsh were thrown from the rooftop while the driver was instantly killed. Rhyce was saved by the white airbag, which was now beet red do to the blood from his broken nose.

The Hummer stopped five feet from falling into the abyss while still resting on its side. For a few seconds everything was oddly quiet and the only movement was the swirling cloud of dust which hovered over the vehicle before curling up towards the cave ceiling and faint sunlight above.

The silence was broken by the faint rustling sound of the immense snake as it slithered through the dirt and began to inspect the overturned vehicle. Unbelievably the Hummer's engine was still running and the snake stopped to sniff the exhaust. With disgust it shook its massive head before swinging it into the back of the vehicle. But instead of pushing the SUV closer to the edge, the force of the blow lifted the Hummer onto two of its wheels, where it tipped back and forth for five seconds before finally landing right side up once again...still sitting only a matter of feet from the edge.

Travis and Amber slowly climbed to their feet surprised the snake hadn't spotted them. Beside Travis the driver's lifeless body lay still in the dirt, but Maddox and Darsh were nowhere to be seen.

Still agitated the long serpent began pushing the Hummer with its head...towards the precipice.

"He's still inside!"

"Let little Rhyce go for a ride."

"Travis! You can't mean-"

He held his hand up and reluctantly nodded his head in agreement.

"Get the others."

She squeezed his arm in thanks and ran into the dark to find Maddox and Darsh while he instead ran towards the snake holding the gun in one hand...and the grenade he had found clipped to the driver's body armour in the other.

The truth was Travis' heroic dash to kill the creature wasn't as altruistic as Amber thought. Yes, he wasn't going to stand by and watch a man die, even a corrupt liar like Rhyce. But he was also trying to save himself and the others. He knew that without the safety of the Hummer the only way any of them would survive for long was to kill the hideous snake, and what better time than now when it was distracted?

Within thirty feet he began firing. Annoyed more than wounded the creature turned its enormous head and instinctively opened its mouth to strike back.

Travis popped the pin with his thumb and threw the grenade with a yell. Despite having been a professional boxer and not a baseball player his aim was perfect and the grenade hurtled straight for the creature's open throat.

But then the snake closed its jaws.

The grenade ricocheted off the creature's closed jawline and rolled along its body until finally dropping into the dirt against the side of the creature's tail forty feet away.

Boom!

The grenade disappeared in a white blaze as it detonated tearing and separating the last five feet of the snake's tail from the rest of its body. The serpent instantly curled its head away from Travis while its thick body shuddered in shock. The snake then coiled all of its body into a tight circle as if to prevent any further damage. Still frightened it then unfurled the four large fins behind its head and wrapped the thick scales around its face for added protection.

Travis resisted the temptation to empty the last clip of the machine gun but decided to instead leap into the shadows and wait. It was a wise move. After waiting for a couple seconds the thick plated scales pulled away from the snake's face and the creature took off, slithering onto the roof of the Hummer before disappearing over the side and down the cliff face into the murky abyss below.

He waited another ten seconds then ran out of the shadows and quickly opened the passenger door. Rhyce's unconscious body slumped halfway out of the SUV, his nose grotesquely warped out of shape with his left eye swelled shut. Travis checked for a pulse and found Rhyce's was still strong. He then looked inside the Hummer and noticed their equipment bags stashed in the cargo compartment while Darsh's bulletproof case was jammed between two of the backseats.

He then heard two familiar but faint voices behind him and turning he saw bobbing flashlights in the distance. Maddox and Amber. He closed the door and ran over to his friends.

Fifty feet away from the Hummer they met and quickly took stock of the situation. Travis explained the grenade blast and condition of Rhyce while Amber relayed that they hadn't found Darsh. Despite a cracked screen her tablet had survived the crash...but there was still no outside signal. Maddox looked as if he had stepped through a grisly tornado. Every piece of clothing or skin was covered in cave grime or torn. Unsurprisingly the copper coloured sunglasses clipped to his shirt were still unscratched.

Despite it all Maddox was grinning but Travis could see the pain behind the smile. He didn't have to guess that his friend's wounded shoulder would be taking a lot longer to heal now.

They began jogging back to the Hummer intent on using the car's high beams to find Darsh, then if still drivable leave before either of the monstrous snakes returned for another attack. As they drew close their flashlights lit up the inside of the SUV. Puzzled Amber said, "I thought you said Rhyce was in the passenger seat."

The Hummer's engine unexpectedly roared and the SUV accelerated forward before suddenly turning and heading directly for the Rebels...a smiling and now alert Rhyce behind the wheel.

They jumped clear in three different directions avoiding the oncoming bumper by only a few feet. Rhyce spun the wheel and did a sluggish turn in the dirt before giving up on the Rebels and instead driving deeper into the darkened cave.

He didn't go far before slamming on the brakes a hundred yards away. He then jumped out of the Hummer and rushed forward beyond the hood of the SUV out of their sight. But in moments they could hear the sound of two voices echoing off the immense cave walls.

Rhyce was arguing with Darsh.

The Rebels jumped to their feet and ran towards the now idling Hummer.

As they got within a dozen steps of the SUV they could see Darsh and Rhyce fighting in front of the grille, the Hummer's lights illuminating every punch and kick. They moved in to intervene but froze as Rhyce threw Darsh into the dirt then pulled a small handgun out of a holster just above his ankle. He then began yelling in a voice that reflected the deep hostility he felt, "Where is the Captain's log book?"

Lying crumpled in the dirt Darsh climbed to his knees his voice stammering, "I thought, thought...we were...we were friends. How could-"

Rhyce pulled the safety back and screamed, "I can't find the treasure without the log book! Where did you put it?"

Darsh shook even more and answered, "I thought...I thought we would find the treasure together...I trusted you!"

Hidden from view Travis and the others quietly began climbing onto the roof of the Hummer where Travis planned to use the machine gun to order Rhyce to surrender. But before he got the chance Rhyce grabbed Darsh by the shoulder and dragged him to the jagged edge of the roadway, where he threw the young adventurer into the dirt only feet from the abyss.

Travis released the trigger and spat into the air in disgust. "No shot from here."

Seventy feet away and certain he was about to die, Darsh became defiant and strong.

"The Treasure Rebels will find the treasure! And justice for me! They-"

A strange malicious smirk crossed Rhyce's bloodstained face as he pointed the gun at Darsh's head.

"No, I'll find some way to get the treasure without the logbook, and your body will be eaten by one of those snakes and you'll be forgotten forever."

They were Rhyce's last words.

Behind him in the darkness the larger of the two snakes re-appeared, and the last sound Rhyce heard was the awful primordial hiss a dozen feet above his head. The creature had taken a striking poise in the shadows of the cave and with a fast strike its jaws shot down and decapitated the arrogant criminal. The rest of Rhyce's body fell over the edge, followed by the monstrous snake who ignored the trembling Darsh completely.

The Rebels immediately jumped off the Hummer to run to Darsh. They didn't take two steps before freezing as the second snake slithered into view behind their new friend! Before they could yell a warning the creature's green teeth snapped onto Darsh's jacket with a loud *clack*. The snake then dragged him across the roadway towards the stone wall.

Travis unloaded every last round in the machine gun at the slithering monster while he and the others jumped into the Hummer and followed the fast moving reptile. As before the bullets couldn't slice through the snake's thick scales, and the snake slinked across the dirt at an incredible speed despite missing the last five feet of its tail from the grenade blast earlier.

Still dragging Darsh the hideous reptile reached the wall. It didn't bite the young adventurer or wrap its long body around him to choke him. Instead it tilted its head upwards......and swallowed him whole.

Inside the vehicle Amber covered her eyes in anguish, "No! No! It's horrible! This is...awful! Turn the car away!"

But the Hummer didn't move. Instead she heard Maddox asking Travis, "You think he's completely swallowed yet?"

She looked up horrified at his words. "We're leaving now!"

She then slapped Travis's shoulder from behind. "Tell him Travis!"

But he ignored her too and continued to watch with Maddox as the snake remained still, wishing to rest having just "eaten."

"Yeah...you can see the outline of his body well past the back teeth. Why?"

"Buckle up."

She sighed in relief. "Thank you! Let's leave this appalling place."

But instead Maddox tapped the flat screen activating the back-up airbag system, smashed the accelerator down with his foot, and the Hummer speeded directly *towards* the resting reptile.

She screamed in equal parts anger and astonishment while Travis instead held on tightly finally understanding Maddox's plan.

The Hummer got closer and closer and only in the final second did the snake slowly turn its head to face the oncoming SUV. A second later Maddox drove the Hummer directly into the creature's head smashing it solidly into the stone wall. The skull was crushed on impact.

Amber looked up covered in glass and surrounded by airbags more stunned than she had ever been before. She couldn't understand why Maddox had just risked their lives to kill an animal they could easily have just driven away from.

But when Maddox and Travis jumped out of the SUV and opened the trunk she finally understood his plan. And her anger completely disappeared.

Outside Maddox and Travis each hoisted the modified chainsaws across their shoulders and approached the snake's unmoving body. They fired the chainsaws up and began cutting into the snake like it was a log of wood. Maddox separated the body from the head which was still pinned to the wall behind the bumper, while Travis cut roughly eight feet down from him. The job complete they rolled the eight foot piece of snake away from the wall...and with great effort pulled Darsh's motionless body out.

He was unresponsive and covered in the snake's digestive juices which had bleached his jet black hair a pale white colour. Amber didn't care and immediately gave him CPR. After a minute she knelt back up and looked at Travis in alarm. It wasn't working.

Then suddenly Darsh began sputtering in a frenzied fit as his lungs gasped for oxygen.

Darsh Bombet was still alive.

With Amber and Travis' help he was carefully lifted into a sitting position against the stone wall. The shock of what he had witnessed and undergone was almost too much for him to handle, unsure whether Rhyce's admission of betrayal, ghastly demise, or his own near death experience distressed him the most. Even worse, it had all happened in less than three minutes!

Amber knelt by his side and examined his eyes and took his pulse while speaking calmly and encouragingly to him. His breathing slowly began returning to normal along with his composure. She turned her head to tell the others the good news that he had no signs of shock and that his pulse was now steady. But Maddox and Travis were already searching the Hummer.

Travis stepped into the driver's seat to find the CB Radio was unresponsive and the engine barely sputtered when he turned the keys. The Hummer appeared dead for good. He then spotted the black case in the backseat covered in shards of glass. He grabbed the handle and lifted it out in one smooth motion before setting it carefully onto the warped hood. In the dim light he then snapped open both latches and lifted the lid...to reveal the three compartments. One filled with an empty glass container, one covered in a velvet cloth, and the final one containing the eighteenth century axe pistol with a large jewel embedded in the bottom of the handle.

Speechless Travis carefully grasped the ancient weapon and lifted it, the emerald green jewel turning the dim light into a colourful green reflection against the black stone wall. He pulled the safety back and heard the ominous click, then carefully pushed the safety back on. He then examined the silver plating on the handle, surprised to see the artwork which was carved into it.

He lifted the old gun into the air and looked back at Maddox who was hoisting the rest of their equipment out of the trunk.

"Pirate axe pistol. Fully preserved."

"Loaded?"

"No, but the axe looks deadly."

Maddox grinned, already arming himself with a new tranquilizer gun and extra cartridges of ammo.

"What else?"

Travis turned back to the case.

"Hold on."

He put the pistol back and lifted the black velvet cloth which covered the item in the centre of the case.

Silence.

A long moment passed and Maddox looked up uneasily. Almost nothing surprised Travis.

"Something crazy?"

Travis shook his head in awe and half mumbled back, "Off the charts wild."

Carrying a new fully charged light Maddox sprinted to the car's hood. There Travis was holding the skull of what appeared to have been a large snake almost the same size as the one now mashed behind the Hummer's front bumper.

Speechless they both looked the artefact over. The skull was about three feet long and two feet wide, and every three inch saw-like tooth was still in place. Amber noticed their stunned silence and after making sure Darsh was still stable she hurried over.

Travis handed her the skull which was surprisingly heavy, much heavier than a bone artefact should be. She quickly put the skull onto the mangled hood and passed her tablet over it, the screen slowly turning red then blue then green.

"You can do that without an outside signal?"

"For scans like this, yes."

The tablet beeped twice and rows of data flashed across the screen.

"Here's the specs guys. Matches the same snake species of the tooth you found earlier. Age of skull is difficult to pinpoint but well over two hundred years old. The entire skull is covered in a plaster like material and the insides of the bone have been filled with steel. Someone clearly preserved the skull hoping it would last forever."

She then tapped the screen until the image was magnified ten times.

"Handwritten on the bottom of the jaw, barely visible beneath any of the plaster and scratched right into the bone is the date 1735. There's also a small dash of artwork...a strange sword."

Travis lifted the pirate pistol out of the case and handed it to her, the dim light reflecting off the carved drawing etched into the silver plating.

"Like this sword symbol?"

"Yes! The *Yeti Slasher's* from Nihar's glass display case!"

She felt the weight of the ancient gun and looked at the axe in disapproval.

"The jewel is beautiful but the axe is dull and chips of the blade are missing."

Travis smiled in approval, "That just means its battle tested."

She handed the old pirate weapon back and pointed at the empty glass container in the case. "Where the log book is supposed to be?"

Maddox pointed at Darsh who was now reading a leather bound book filled with parchment paper. "Looks like Darsh took the book with him when he left the Ferrari. Must have been carryin' it the whole time."

Travis replied, "Would've loved to see Rhyce's face when he stole the case only to see the book was missing when he opened it!"

Amber then noticed their equipment bag lying open near the Hummer. It appeared empty.

"Did much of our gear survive?"

Maddox handed her an extra tranquilizer gun loaded with one clip and another flashlight. "This is all that's left."

She nodded her head and looked out into the cave as she tapped the vehicle's damaged hood.

"Let's use the Hummer for armoured shelter. I don't like waiting out here worrying that snake monster will return."

Travis locked the case with the two items returned and nodded, "I'll carry Darsh to the car."

They then turned to Maddox but he was already thirty feet away into the blackness of the tunnel.

"Maddox!"

He turned back and grinned, "Back in two minutes."

Before they could argue he was gone, the light from his LED light already swallowed by the sombre darkness of the mountain cave.

Annoyed Amber rushed over to Darsh while Travis leaned into the Hummer and carefully slid the black case onto one of the back seats. He then froze as a strange sizzling sound echoed from within the SUV.

The CB Radio was back to life.

He dove behind the steering wheel and began trying every frequency.

Static.

He gritted his teeth in frustration and tried every channel a second time, calling out for assistance into the mike.

Finally a faint voice broke through the garbled static acknowledging Travis.

It was Nihar.

Before Travis could reply he explained he was well and had received the proper anti-venom in time.

When there was a brief pause Travis quickly replied, "We've kept our promise. We have Darsh."

"Is he all right? Does he seem well?"

Travis looked through the passenger window at Darsh who was being helped to his feet. He was unsteady but now actually smiling a little, holding onto the pirate journal as if it were a winning lottery ticket.

"He'll be fine...except for the phobia of snakes he'll have forever now."

Nihar paused in fear as he reflected on what Travis' words might mean.

"No! He did not get bitten did he? Please tell me now!"

"Well, uh, *bitten* ain't really the right word."

"I do not understand. Does he need anti-venom?"

"Just a good bath and some black hair dye for a week."

Nihar choked on the green tea he was drinking until he sputtered, "What? I don't..."

"Darsh is healthy enough. He'll be okay."

Nihar simply sighed in relief, "My gratitude to you and your two friends cannot be put into words Mr. Jagson! May I now speak with Rhyce to coordinate?"

Travis hesitated. Would hearing of Rhyce's betrayal or death shock Nihar more?

"Sit down sir, then I'll explain about Rhyce."

===

Maddox ran as quickly as he could, thankful the dirt muffled the sound of every step. His running into the shadows away from the safety of the SUV seemed foolhardy but he had a good reason. With the Hummer destroyed he figured they would have to eventually abandon it and walk back to the main tunnel...on foot. An easy target if the remaining monstrous serpent returned. And even if they did make it back they would have to scramble through the snake infested tunnels with limited tranquilizer darts and no anti-venom.

He knew the tunnel road had to end at some point and that Rhyce and his men had been travelling in this direction for some reason. He hoped an escape leading to the outside, or at the least an exit from the tunnel road, was only minutes away in the darkness.

After a half minute of hard running the bobbing light reflected the end of the cave road...but no exit. Instead the roadway cut to the right becoming a very small tunnel with stone wall now on both sides. The new tunnel opened up into another narrow cave, with a shaft of light shining down onto the floor through a large opening over a hundred feet above. The cave itself was only about three hundred square feet wide, and vacant except for a skeleton sitting against one of the walls flanked by two muskets half buried in the dirt.

The skeleton was wearing a thick jacket made of brownish white fur, complete with a hoodie that covered the top of the scowling skull. Beneath the jacket were the thin ragged remains of sailors breeches covering the leg bones and only the straps of what had been leather boots over the feet. But despite a thick coating of dust and dirt the fur jacket had barely begun to wear away despite the passage of time.

His initial uneasiness at the sight of the skeleton now gone, Maddox stepped closer and turned the light to have a better look at the bony remains.

What he saw spooked even him.

The jacket had been torn across the right side and behind the tear he could see four of the skeleton's ribs had been broken in two. Clearly a fatal blow. After seeing what had happened to Rhyce his first thought was that another monstrous serpent was likely responsible for the man's death. But in the light the tear and broken ribs looked too clean for a messy animal bite. If anything it looked more like a slash from a claw.

He turned away from the gruesome sight and was surprised by what the LED light revealed next.

In one of the skeleton's curled bony fingers was a quill pen. He looked closer and expected to find pieces of paper or an old book, anything that the dying man would have used to write on. But there was nothing in the dirt except the old quill. And footprints.

At least ten prints were visible in the dirt around the skeleton, and in each track were the noticeable treads of modern hiking boots. He stood and followed the tracks to see where they led, guessing that they belonged to mountaineers who had climbed into and out of the cave from the opening high above. But his guess was wrong as the stone wall showed no signs of having been punctured with modern climbing equipment.

He paused and looked up at the open sky his mind churning. Whoever the tracks belonged to they hadn't entered the cave from the main tunnel. If anything he figured they had rappelled down from above, stole items off the skeleton then quickly were lifted back out. Plus they had refused to investigate beyond the small cave which was little more than a dead end.

He then looked back at the spine-chilling skeleton and a new thought struck him. What if the thieving "mountaineers" had been wrong? What if the small cave wasn't a dead end?

He hurried back to the bony remains and paused before the first of the two muskets resting half buried in the dirt, the stocks sticking out a couple feet beside the skeleton's head. He hesitated unsure if he should proceed with his new plan. Wild thoughts of booby traps from adventure movies filled his mind, but he considered the alternative of walking back through the tunnels and caves an even bigger risk.

He made his decision, grasped the mahogany stock of the musket closest to him, and with a grunt he tried to pry it loose.

=======================================

In the Hummer Travis listened as Nihar voiced his outrage at Rhyce's betrayal and attempt at killing his son. In a rare show of chilling rage Nihar spat, "I wish I could have been in that cave to watch Rhyce die."

Travis paused, uneasy and unsure how to respond.

Nihar instead continued, "Pardon my angry words Mr. Jagson. Strong feelings from an angry father that is all. Has Darsh spoken of me yet?"

Travis pushed the mike button and replied, "Not yet. He's still a bit stunned, but he's safe."

"Where are you now? Is the snake still nearby?"

Travis intently looked up at the reflection in the rear view mirror which showed nothing but the darkness of the cave beyond. He then looked out the passenger window and saw Amber helping Darsh slowly walk towards the SUV. Travis lifted the mike to reply.

"No sign since the last attack. Looks like we're gonna wait it out inside the Hummer till help arrives."

"Can you drive it closer to the entry doors?"

"Without a tow truck it'll never move again."

"That is fine! Nothing will stop me and my men from coming to your rescue now! Can you see a large blue button on the dashboard near the Radio?"

Travis leaned closer and sure enough found the button with the white letters SOS printed on it.

"Hit the button Mr. Jagson. It will send out a beacon signal and my men will be able to find you in the cave."

Travis hit the button and it immediately filled with light.

"You gettin' the signal?"

"I have it Mr. Jagson! Tell the others I can't wait to thank them for finding Darsh! You all stay in the Hummer. Twenty minutes."

"Tell your men to keep eyes out for the snake. But hurry. Your Hummer can't shield us forever from that thing."

"Do not worry Treasure Rebels. I am coming to get you and my son!"

With that static filled the cabin as the wealthy man from New Delhi signed out. Travis replaced the mike and jumped out to help Amber who was now just a few feet from one of the passenger doors on the other side of the SUV.

But before he had taken two steps he noticed the LED light bobbing in the distance and getting closer. In seconds Maddox appeared, the usual confident smile on his face.

"Good news?"

"Got Nihar on the CB. He and his boys are on the way, turned out there's a tracking beacon inside the Hummer. He says twenty minutes. Found anything fun during your stroll?"

"Just a skeleton wearing a hoodie, likely guarding treasure."

Together they then found Amber helping the young treasure hunter the last few steps to the SUV. She looked up relieved to see them, now filled with fatigue at supporting much of Darsh's weight.

Darsh grasped the top of the vehicle's roof to steady himself as Maddox stepped in to support his other arm. Travis hurriedly opened the door and spoke.

"Good news buddy, your dad is coming to rescue you!"

Darsh suddenly stood up straight, almost falling backwards in disbelief, his expression full of unbelieving anxiety.

Then looking at each of the Treasure Rebels he answered chillingly.

"My father died three years ago."

PART III: THE SKELETON'S HANDWRITING

Darsh shook free and stepped backwards in a panic, his eyes filled with furious anger and mistrust.

"Both of my parents died in a boating accident in the Indian Ocean! This...this is sick trick!"

He then marched back towards them and grasped Maddox across the shoulders with both hands shouting angrily, "Who do you really work for? Tell me!"

The Rebels stood still, completely unsure how to reply to such a shocking statement. The easy answer was that Darsh had lost his senses. That he had suffered some sort of head injury or that the stress of weeks of being trapped in the Himalayan cave or even the dangers of the last hour had broken his mind.

But Darsh's eyes reflected a young man whose mind was perfectly clear. They knew he was telling the truth and their shock at Darsh's outburst was replaced with a chill of alarm they had never experienced before.

The Rebels had battled many types of criminals over the last two years as they had travelled the world. Professional thieves, forgers, black market dealers, even amoral men willing to kill for treasure. But no enemy like Nihar. And no situation like this.

"Darsh we were hired by this man. He helped find Maddox in a South American jungle and asked us to find you as a return favour for his good deed."

Amber then handed Darsh the tablet with a picture of Nihar filling the screen.

"We even visited his mansion in New Delhi. He picked us up in a limousine and showed us his collection of military artefacts. There was even a recording he played of you calling him for help."

She then tapped the screen which revealed the photos she had taken of Nihar's study and the supercars around the fountain.

Darsh looked at the images in silence, his face growing sadder with each picture. He then looked up from the screen and spoke.

"That is Nihar Archer. He is a shipping owner from Mumbai and is not related to my family lineage in any way. He was a business partner of Rhyce. He provided special boat and two man crew in Bay of Bengal so we could scuba dive to recover the case. But I never call him or anyone else for help, my phone was broken at the car crash."

He then slumped down against the Hummer in misery.

"That is *my* house and *my* artifacts and cars! Nihar owns **none** of it! I see now not only was Rhyce using me but Nihar as well. I am a fool."

Maddox handed him another canteen of water and asked, "How did you know where to dive?"

"Rhyce knew."

Amber nervously looked behind the SUV for any signs of the snake then spoke, "How did you meet Rhyce?"

"Through my girlfriend. She works in film production in Mumbai, and when she saw on tv that Rhyce Tucker was going to visit and film in India, she suggested I contact him and see if he could help me recover the Yeti Pirate's treasure. Not only did Rhyce say yes, he told me he knew of shipwreck which was rumoured to hold a journal written by one of the pirates from long ago. A book which described where the pirates had found the mythical treasure."

He sipped water from the canteen, visibly sicker at the memories then his physical injuries. He continued, "I have researched, studied, and collected items around the world which not only proved the Yeti Pirates were real, but I discovered the treasure was stored in this maze of caves filled with snakes. The pirate logbook was like a treasure map, guiding us through the maze. Everything was prepared, I even brought the Ferrari in case we ran into dangerous rivals or if the pirate tales of giant snakes or even the Yeti were true and we needed to escape quickly."

He then drank the rest of the water and weakly tossed the canteen which bounced against the wall. "I did not really believe the snakes were real, but I suspected for months that thieves were tracking us. Now I realize the entire time it was Rhyce and Nihar! But I also see that Rhyce was just a shallow thief, but Nihar stole something much worse...my Father's identity."

Travis stepped away from the SUV and Darsh for a second to collect his thoughts. His hands were clenched into fists and he resisted the urge to punch a hole through one of the Hummer's windows. He had never liked Nihar. Not from the second he and Amber had met him on the beach in Brazil right up to the moment Nihar had left them in the cave, his bloodied arm waving goodbye through the car window at them.

He involuntarily cracked his knuckles the way he used to in the locker room before a boxing match as he thought about the man who had led them into this hellish cave. Nihar was the worst kind of crook. He knew the best way to trick the Rebels hadn't been to promise them a rich payoff of gold, but to instead make them feel indebted to him and abuse their sense of goodwill. Travis had sensed instinctively that Nihar might be running some sort of scam. He never could have guessed the scam was Nihar himself. Travis knew he would never ignore his instincts again.

He then thought back to the CB Radio and spat in disgust at the thought of Nihar laughing at his ignorance as they had talked.

He then snapped back to attention and called out to the others.

"Turn off the beacon in the car!"

He ran past the bumper to instead see the others walking away from the SUV, Amber helping Darsh while Maddox carried the black case.

Maddox shook his head, "Keep the beacon on! We want Nihar and his crew to come here!"

Travis didn't ask why, already remembering Maddox's comment about the "skeleton wearing a hoodie" waiting for them in the distance.

Travis didn't hesitate and quickly joined them as they left the Hummer, the dead snake, and the spent chainsaws behind in the shadows.

"Let me carry the case."

Five minutes later they reached the small cave, Maddox's light illuminating the eerie remains of the Yeti Pirate. Half stunned Darsh carefully examined the pirate bones and hoodie, his mouth open in shock but unable to say anything. He then noticed the quill pen in the skeletal hand.

Excitedly he pointed to the log book in his own hand, "This is the pirate who wrote the logbook. The Captain!"

"How can you be sure?"

"I am sure Miss Amber! Because he explained right in the book that he lay dying just like this!" He then began hurriedly turning the pages to find the quotation. But before he could find the correct page Maddox stepped forward and pulled the musket to the right of the skeleton completely out of the ground. A strange sound like that of rusted gears turning against one another filled the air until the rock face to the left of the skeleton began to move leaving a small opening roughly three feet wide and four feet high.

Without hesitation Maddox entered still carrying the pirate musket.

As the others followed Darsh looked at the rock face in trepidation.

"What if it closes behind us?"

Up ahead Maddox replied, "It won't until the musket is put back in the ground."

Darsh grinned but then paused as an eerie sound reached his ears. The sound of a car's exhaust could be heard approaching from above. The Rebels heard it too and Travis urged Darsh to catch up with them. "It's probably Nihar!"

"How? He couldn't have known about this place, not even I knew!"

All four hurriedly ran deeper into the small tunnel as fast as possible. The temperature became colder, the stone walls became a lighter blue colour, and the sound of the vehicle's engine outside was replaced with the faded echo of bubbling water in the distance.

"Can you get a better signal yet?"

Amber turned to Travis and shook her head, "Only for a few seconds. Not enough time to get a call through for help."

They soon had to slow down as the stone path became a cluttered mess of puddles and icy mud.

Maddox suddenly looked at Darsh intensely.

"Did the pirates leave behind booby traps to protect their treasure?"

"I read most of the journal while in the Ferrari. There was no mention of any traps. But I will re-read the last section which the pirate Captain wrote!"

Darsh then quickly opened the battered ancient book and turned to the last few pages as he and the Treasure Rebels cautiously continued forward. Amber tapped the side of her tablet and a small penlight slid out. "Here, you can use this for light to read." He took the metallic pen and using the bright light found the correct page. He then read aloud the Yeti Pirate Captain's last words which had been written over two hundred years before:

"I'm bleedin' out...The doctor still thinks I have a chance but I know better...The claw went right through my chest, tore clean through some of my ribs...when I try to stand I can feel some of my chest bones move in the wrong direction...I will never be able to stand up again, my restin' place will be here outside the creature's den. As per my last orders, the men will seal the opening and leave me be, then use the timber to cover over the passageway near the cave entrance...the doctor keeps pushing the strong rum on me, thinks it will dull the pain. The fool! The pain cutting through my bones is nothing compared to the guilt I feel for bringin' the men here. We knew the stories were true, but I listened to my stupid

pride and not my good sense. Thought the Yeti would fall quickly to a round of musket fire...I was wrong. I even put a round directly into the creature's leg. But every shot only made the crazed animal angrier...more starving it seemed."

Darsh turned the page before looking up at Maddox and the others who were staring at him in amazement. They had stopped moving and were instead waiting for him to continue reading. He hurriedly looked back down at the yellow faded page:

"Thirty-one! Thirty-one good men dead! I led the crew right into the creature's lair! Only three men will escape here, the rest are already dead. My responsibility! I never should have let that depraved merchant talk me into coming here. The other Yetis were smaller, less violent. He never told me this one was twice the height of a man...and with...those awful spikes! He promised me our greatest gain, instead we lost everything...We cannot even bury the men at sea as they deserve but must leave them behind...I have instructed the three survivors to hire my uncle the painter, to show in detail what happened here. It is my last hope that the painting will serve as a warning to keep other hunters such as us from foolishly trying to kill the beast. I can only hope the stories the merchant spread of the treasure fade forever. The creature is not the myth, the treasure is...because the Yeti was the treasure! No Yeti fur to bring back to the merchant, no payment of silver. As for the three survivors, the Doctor, the Gunner, and 'Spikes' the Locksmith...if they make it past the snakes and escape I am confident they will easily evade and sail through the British blockade waiting for them near home...and that they will deliver to my uncle the commission for the painting. What they do with the rest of the coins from our previous expeditions is up to

them...May God forgive me for my failures...The men have just successfully sealed the entrance behind me using my own musket as the lever...I will now shake their hands and wish them Godspeed."

Darsh closed the journal and looked up, his expression one of alarm and remorse.

"There is no treasure in the cave! I believed a lie...a terrible arrogant lie all this time. I...I should have..."

Amber interrupted him and grasped his shoulder while Maddox and Travis were already running back towards the pirate skeleton. "Forget the treasure Nihar! We now have proof the Yeti is real, we've got to get out of this deathtrap!"

"But the Yeti would be over two hundred years old, I doubt a creature could-"

She pushed him towards the others. "Just run Darsh!"
Click click.

They all froze as the faded sounds of machine guns being loaded with ammunition clips reached their ears. A moment later a gust of wind swirled through the tunnel followed by the clear echo of hushed anxious voices.

Nihar's men were inside the tunnel and moments away from reaching them.

With no other choice they ran in the opposite direction, hoping that the mythical creature which had ripped the pirates to pieces centuries ago was not waiting for them. The tunnel twisted left, then right, then after another minute of hard running through the mud the faint sound of voices faded completely behind them. Nihar's men were thankfully moving forward slowly and cautiously.

The tunnel suddenly ended and opened up into a massive cave different than any they had seen before. They shone their lights in every direction to reveal a fifty foot wide body of cold water in the very centre. Everywhere they turned the frosted bones of a skeleton on the cave floor reflected back the light, but not a single silver or gold coin. Most of the stones were black while a handful reflected a light blue coating of frosted ice. The cave floor was uneven and filled with small stones, large boulders, and hardened mud. To their right a shaft of bright light shined down from a narrow opening in the stone ceiling eighty feet above. It was the only way out.

Except for Maddox they had all seen the cave depicted before in the oil painting.

They were in the Yeti lair.

They stepped into the lair unconsciously holding their breath for a few moments in uneasiness. The only sounds to be heard was the gurgling water as it splashed against the black rocks lining the pool and the crunch of their boots atop the frost covered pebbled mud. The tension was unlike anything they had experienced before.

Without a word Maddox signalled they walk towards the stone wall to their right. Climbing out was the only option. But after a few careful steps they stopped as a new sound ricocheted off the walls and reached their ears.

The echo of a large animal lapping up water.

They looked towards the source of the sound two hundred feet away...and their blood chilled in disbelieving dread.

PART IV: THE MYTH REVEALED

The mythical Yeti.

Resting on its two legs and arms like a bear it was slowly drinking the cold water on the other side of the pool. Covered in dirt the Yeti had almost blended into the cave's dark surroundings. It looked about the size of a large bull and had four black eight inch claws protruding from its front paws as it held onto the black rocks.

The Rebels and Darsh watched in growing terror as the mythical creature turned its head as its black eyes finally noticed them. The purple black tongue disappeared back inside its grizzled hairy jaws and with a deep grunt it sluggishly stood and began to walk slowly on its hind legs toward them. After a dozen steps the beast stepped into the sunlight and they got to see the legendary creature clearly.

About twelve feet tall while standing on its hind legs, the Yeti's body was covered in the same brownish white fur of the pirate hoodies. Its immense feet resembled a cross between the paws of a polar bear and a human foot, and its arms were tucked closely to its sides as it walked. In the clear light the eight inch black front claws were visibly curved like those of a jaguar.

Unlike the myths reported in the news the face did not resemble a human being. Instead it looked like a cross between a gorilla and a polar bear. The nose was long and pointed, thin white fur covered most of its head, while grayish wispy fur hung off its face and chin resembling a grotesque, almost humorous goatee beard. There were no visible ears like those of an ape and its tongue rested at the side of its mouth like that of a panting tired dog.

Every step seemed to be an effort and in the eerie stillness they could hear the creature straining for breath. It was also slightly dragging its right leg, and despite its frightening height the Yeti appeared underweight, with patches of the fur on its legs, chest, and right leg thinning out. As the Yeti grew closer they could see the cause of the thinning fur were multiple scars...gunshot and knife wounds from the battle with pirates over two hundred years before.

The Rebels and Darsh slowly began stepping backwards as the creature lifted its arms in anger and let out a primal grunt now only fifty feet away. It then lowered its arms and simply stood still watching them, constantly favouring the right leg with the musket ball from the pirate Captain still embedded in the kneecap.

A brief flash of hope passed through their minds. Perhaps the creature was not interested in attack, perhaps it was now simply too old and crippled to be a real threat, and would leave all four of them alone once they were clear of its territory.

But the Yeti shattered the quiet as it suddenly lifted both of its arms above its head once again and unleashed the loudest roar they had ever heard from any animal. As the beast screamed they could see its teeth were not white but black, and like that of a rabid dog saliva was gushing out at the sides of its mouth.

It then ran right towards them as fast as an enraged grizzly.

Before they could properly react the Yeti swung one of its paws at Travis who barely lifted the case up to his face to protect himself in time. The claws struck the bulletproof steel and drove Travis off his feet up into the air towards the left side of the lair. The force of the strike was unlike anything he had experienced as a pro boxer and he landed stunned twenty five feet away in the mud, the case now sliced open and in shattered pieces beside him.

The Yeti then turned and swung towards Maddox and Amber but missed as the two treasure hunters rolled to safety behind a large boulder. But the creature's immense hand struck the dirt where they had been standing and the force of the impact caused Darsh to stumble backwards into the mud only ten feet away from the Yeti's slavering jaws.

The beast's narrow black eyes set on Darsh until five darts embedded deep into the exposed skin of the Yeti's face. The beast turned towards Maddox and Amber who fired every remaining dart into the creature's chin and fur covered throat.

The cave beast responded with another wild howl and with a leap jumped ten feet through the air and swung its right arm at their faces. They both dove for the cold mud and the eight inch claws missed their heads by a couple feet, leaving a two inch deep slice into the face of the boulder instead.

The beast then turned its head to look at Darsh who was struggling in fright to get to his feet. The creature howled again and in the sunlight the long claws could be seen twitching as the Yeti prepared to deliver a death blow.

But Maddox was even angrier. Jumping to his feet he lifted the old musket from behind his back and leaped, rolling to a stop in front of the beast. Without stopping he lifted the musket and brought the butt down as hard as he could directly into the Yeti's damaged knee.

An ear-splitting *crack* filled the cave as the old weapon smacked directly into the Yeti's bone. Maddox then dove through the beast's legs and lifted the musket to deliver a second blow to the back of the Yeti's leg. But as he lifted the ancient gun he realized the beast's knee hadn't cracked in two...the musket had.

Holding the splintered gun in his hands he looked up stunned as the Yeti reached down and grabbed him by his injured shoulder. Then with rage filled ease the creature hurled him forty feet across the cave into the mud filled shadows near the stone wall on the right side.

The Yeti then roared as if to taunt Maddox, the black purple tongue sloshing back and forth in its mouth. When Maddox didn't move the Yeti stepped towards Amber and in so doing its fleshy hairy foot stepped onto Maddox's sunglasses which had fallen into the chilled mud.

Amber slowly stepped back in dread as the twelve foot beast closed in. She had no weapons and could never outrun the creature.

Behind the Yeti Travis slowly stood, the smashed remnants of the black case at his feet. He knew there was only one way to save Amber. He had to fight the beast off. He looked down and pulled the pistol out of the muck. The axe blade was missing. He holstered the ancient weapon on the side of his leg anyway. Then he saw it. The snake skull.

He kicked aside the broken pieces of the case and lifted the bone artefact up. Then he remembered the inside of the skull had been filled with steel. And in the dim light he could see a metal ring in the inside centre that would have been used to hang the skull in a display case. He reached inside and grasped the handle. It was a perfect fit. He could use the fearsome skull as a sort of primitive shield and striking weapon all at the same time.

He immediately began yelling at the Yeti and with fury he threw a piece of the case directly towards the back of the beast's head. Direct hit.

The beast roared and spun its head to see Travis taunting and shouting. The Yeti dropped back onto all fours and charged directly at him.

Travis then yelled to Amber while readying himself for the fight, "Help them!"

She wanted to disagree but knew he was right. She rushed over to help Darsh up then together they ran towards Maddox who was slowly beginning to climb to his feet at the base of the stone wall. Darsh suddenly lifted his arm as something caught his eye reflecting in the mountain sunlight.

"Wait Miss Amber!"

As she watched puzzled he stooped down and lifted Maddox's copper coloured sunglasses out of the mud. Inexplicably the Yeti's full weight hadn't broken or even bent the shades. Without a word they continued on to Maddox, afraid to look back at what could be a slaughter behind them.

The Yeti reached Travis, jumped back on its hind feet and swung its right claw at his forehead. Travis ducked and swung back with the skull in a vicious uppercut motion. He actually had to jump to reach the Yeti's head and with a booming sound the polished bone and embedded steel of the snake's skull directly smashed into the beast's lower face. The Yeti's body barely moved but its head snapped to the side and a small stream of blood and four black teeth splattered onto the stones below.

One for Travis.

But then the Yeti responded with a vertical slash downwards with its other arm, the curved claws heading directly towards the top of his head. Travis lifted the skull at the last millisecond and the claws embedded right through the top of the snake skull, only stopped by the steel inside. The Yeti immediately tried to pull its claws free as Travis held firmly onto the ring inside the skull.

He then stepped in close and unleashed his hardest left cross as deeply as he could into the creature's stomach hoping to damage some vulnerable tissue.

A bone did break, but it was part of Travis' hand.

One for the Yeti.

The beast then lifted its hairy left foot and kicked Travis directly in the chest. The force of the violent blow sent him flying backwards and pulled the skull free of the Yeti's claw at the same time. Travis quickly stumbled to his feet covered in grimy mud and lifted the skull defensively, but he was coughing violently and his chest shook in spasms as he couldn't breathe.

Two for the Yeti.

The cave beast continued to attack, leaping forward and drilling both monstrous arms down directly like clubs. Travis barely avoided what would have been a lethal strike. But the incredible force of the Yeti's clawed paws slamming into the stones at Travis' feet threw the treasure hunter backwards, where he smacked into the cave wall and sliced the skin at the back of his head.

Three for the Yeti.

As Travis struggled to stand the Yeti closed in and began to raise one of its arms in a swinging motion to deliver the final death strike. But the whole time Travis had never let go of the skull. With his back literally to the wall this was his last chance...or his last moments alive.

With a yell he leaped and struck the Yeti again directly across the beast's large forehead. The already damaged snake skull vibrated at the impact and Travis felt as if his hand had turned to mush for a second. But the blow caused the Yeti to step back a couple paces briefly disoriented, and Travis had a clear shot at the beast's kneecap.

With a yell full of adrenaline he drove the snake skull squarely into the side of the Yeti's knee, driving the fossilized snake teeth deep into the cartilage and bone.

Two for Travis.

The Yeti bayed in shock and took two more steps back, which pulled the skull out of Travis' hand as the snake teeth were now jammed into the knee bone. The howl of pain turned into a howl of rage and the beast lifted both of its arms in a threatening posture...and a set of three black spikes suddenly appeared out of the fur in both forearms, each spike an incredible two feet long and as sharp as the dangerous edge of a razor.

Travis didn't have time to stare in wonder at the astounding sight. Instead he pulled the axe pistol out of the holster just as the Yeti swung the spikes at his head with both arms in a scissor like motion. He ducked at the last second and could hear the hiss of the spikes as they cut through the chilled mountain air inches above his scalp. He then rolled forward and stabbed downward, driving the pointed edge of the green jewel deep into the exposed skin on the top of the Yeti's foot as hard as he could.

Three for Travis.

The Yeti rolled away in agony now severely weakened and barely able to move.

This was Travis' moment.

Despite barely breathing he stood, leaped over a mangled pirate skeleton, and ran across the lair to join the others. They saw him coming and began the climb up the wall towards sunlight and freedom above. A moment later he almost tripped and collapsed when his right boot clipped a skeleton foot sticking out of the cold mud. But he regained his balance in mid stride and reaching the wall he began to climb at an incredible speed only a dozen feet below the others.

Maddox and Amber looked down and yelled back encouragement while Darsh simply kept climbing, his whole attention focused on not losing his already feeble grip. It was a good thing he hadn't looked down.

Now visible below them in the clear water the outline of the monstrous snake became visible as the fifty-foot reptile swam towards the surface. Within seconds its hideous glowing teeth broke clear of the water and the serpent began to slither into the Yeti lair.

Closest to the ground Travis was the first to hear the hissing and he spotted the serpent. He then turned his eyes away from the curling snake and stole a quick look back at the Yeti which was slowly pulling the jewel out of its fleshy foot...growling in agony at the effort. He then turned back to climbing while the others were almost at the very top, their hands already stretching into the Himalayan sunlight. Both creatures below seemed uninterested in following them and in seconds they would be free. Everything looked good.

Then everything went wrong.

An odd clinking sound echoed throughout the cave which sounded like aluminum cans bouncing and rolling along the stones.

Panic filled Travis' eyes as he recognized the sound. He looked back down and just glimpsed the form of one of Nihar's men jumping for cover behind a boulder. He looked up and only had time to utter one word of warning to the others who were just beginning to pull themselves out the cave.

"*Grenades!*"

Four distinct blasts one after the other shook every stone and the darkened cave was illuminated with flaming orange light. Twenty more skeletons of the Yeti Pirates which had been hidden in the shadows were now briefly visible.

The blast wave hurled Darsh and Amber out of the cave onto the pale green grass of the Himalayan countryside.

Maddox was instead thrown backwards plummeting downwards towards the cave floor until he grabbed an outcropping of stone with his right hand. He momentarily stopped until the stone crumbled in his hand and he dropped the last twenty feet to the bottom hitting the ground hard.

Because he was closest to the grenades Travis was affected by the force of the blast the worst of all of them. In a smoke filled blur he was tossed away from the wall flipping end over end until he hit the pool of water and disappeared submerged from view.

But the monstrous snake suffered a direct hit. The original target of the grenades, it curled into a ball as the blast tore off part of its lower jaw. Stunned and bleeding it began hissing furiously then swivelled and slithered back into the water. Right where Travis had fallen in.

When Nihar's men stepped from behind their hiding positions and began firing they expected to face the fifty foot serpent. Instead what they saw was the Yeti galloping on all fours directly towards them, its wounded foot and leg barely slowing it down as rage filled adrenaline coursed through its old body. Not a single grenade had exploded near the beast, so all the explosions had done was push the Yeti into a livid frenzy where it felt no pain.

Nihar's three men frantically fired off a dozen rounds. The Yeti stopped, stood, and with a primal yell astonishingly shook its fur until every bullet popped out and dropped to the stones at its feet.

There was no second round of firing.

Instead each criminal ran in the opposite direction heaving more grenades at the Yeti to cover their escape. The Yeti hesitated as three of the grenades rolled to a stop near its clawed feet. The creature didn't understand what a grenade was...but it instinctively sensed lethal danger.

With a snort it turned and clawing the ground hurried in the other direction leaping into the water as well...just before the grenades exploded. Kicking both of its legs the Yeti swam deeper into the depths.

Towards Travis and the dinosaur sized snake.

==

Amber shook her head, brushed strands of red hair away from her eyes, then slowly rolled to her side and looked up at the skyline and the rows of Himalayan mountain tops in the distance. With the mountain peaks shrouded in curling mist and the blue sky filled with light falling snow the view was both magnificent and timeless.

The quiet moment ended as the sound of the three grenades exploding from deep within the cave reached her ears. But before she could react another sound cut through the mountain air this time from above.

Helicopters.

She faintly hoped that somehow the police had tracked her unsuccessful tablet calls. But she knew better.

Nihar.

Three hundred feet away two green helicopters slowly descended onto the frozen tundra of the Himalayan hillside she stood on. She could see Nihar staring out through one of the cockpit windows. As he stepped free of the chopper she saw his arm was covered in clean bandages and he showed no signs of any ill health.

Walking beside the conman were two of his men both carrying handguns. She lifted her arms slowly in surrender as they approached while off in the distance Nihar's last Hummer could be seen driving onto the hilltop. Inside were the three mercenaries who had just escaped from the Yeti lair below.

Nihar slowed down and pointed at something to his right. The two men nodded their heads and jogged over to a stretch of long grass where Darsh was slowly struggling to stand. In one hand he held Amber's tablet and in the other the pirate logbook. The two armed "guards" grabbed him by the shoulders and dragged him until they threw him onto the ground beside Amber.

The Hummer pulled onto the snowy grass and parked. The men quickly ran over to their boss in a frightened panic.

Nihar listened quietly as they excitedly told him about the Yeti and snake, their eyes still filled with frightened shock at what they had seen in the cave. Once finished Nihar pointed at Amber and Darsh and asked his men a question. All three shrugged their shoulders. Whatever the question was they didn't know.

He then turned away from them and angrily strode across the grass until he was standing over his two prisoners.

"Where is Tarver and Jagson?"

==

Far below Maddox shook his head as consciousness returned. He slowly stood and groaned at the new jolt of raw pain coming from the injured shoulder. The last things he remembered were Travis yelling, the grenade blast, the painful fall, and the image of his good friend flying into the water.

He didn't hesitate. He ignored the pain and jumped headfirst into the mysterious pool of water as well.

==

Outside and far above the pool Nihar was losing his patience.

"Where is Maddox Tarver!!"

Darsh looked up and sputtered a convincing lie, "The Yeti ate him."

The conman looked sharply at Amber.

"And what about the former boxer?"

She looked up and lied as well.

"Grenades."

He stepped away from them satisfied with their answers. He stared into the clouds for a long pause before turning back to them, his face a strange combination of smugness and antagonism.

"Rather ironic I never got to meet Mr. Tarver is it not?"

He then stepped over to the open crevice and looked down into the cave smiling. "He would have been better off had I left him in the jungle with those natives."

He then nervously tugged at his goatee and his voice grew chillingly cold.

"How did Rhyce die?"

Despite shaking from the growing cold Darsh replied clearly, "The big snake." Then he got defiant, "Ironic he left me to die in that cave and in the end it is him who gets eaten."

Nihar continued tugging nervously at his goatee and was about to reply but Darsh continued, "But you are the real monster. My father was a man of honour. The world will see who you are...you will not bring false disgrace on my family name."

Nihar smugly ignored Darsh and instead studied the tablet. Suddenly he looked up in concern as he saw the number Amber had been trying to call. "You called the police?" But before she could respond he said, "It doesn't matter...it will take the Indian authorities hours to find this mountain hilltop."

Amber smiled back and lied, "I gave them directions to the mansion."

He froze as his eyes bulged in panic. Paralyzing anxiety turned into frightened anger and walking over to the crevice he *threw* the tablet as hard as he could into the cave below. Now out of sight the tablet spun threw the air until it splashed into the pool of water and sank beneath the surface.

Nihar then pulled out a handgun of his own and pointed it at Darsh.

"The Yeti was real so the pirate treasure must be real as well. My men didn't see a single gold coin or gold bar down there...where is it!"

Darsh knew that telling the conman the truth that the pirates were only after the Yeti's fur hide and not money would result in a bullet to his chest. So he instead came up with another convincing lie.

"The treasure was not stored in the cave. Instead the location is secretly written in the painting. With the logbook as a guide I can find the coordinates for you."

To seem more convincing he handed Nihar the pirate logbook.

"The pirate Captain wrote it all in there."

Amber watched Nihar grab the old leather book, her digital pen still attached to the yellowed pages.

He briefly scanned the book and a strange ugly smile appeared across his tired face. "I never got to read the logbook when Rhyce and I first found it in that tiny cave with the skeleton Captain. At the time we thought the cave was little more than a dead end, so we took everything we could use, the logbook, the pistol, even an old dinosaur skull and left. Painfully we lost everything in the Bay a few days later during a storm," He smirked at Darsh and continued, "But thanks to you, you helped retrieve it all for me! I'm certain you are right that the secrets to the treasure's location are in these pages."

The conman then pocketed the pirate logbook and called out to his men, "We're heading back to the mansion to grab the painting!"

He then smiled wickedly at Amber while pointing condescendingly at Darsh, "Goodbye Miss Monette. Without your help I never would have been able to track down this pitiful daydreamer." He then turned away and began running towards the helicopters while yelling at his men. "Bring him!"

The mercenaries paused and pointed at Amber. "What about the redhead?"

He paused and looked at the nearby cliff face to their right which overlooked the hilltop. A rolling cloud of fog was moving across the hanging stones and in the far distance a faint wolf howl could be heard. "She has nowhere to go, only the wolves up here to keep her company. Leave her!"

Darsh quickly turned to Amber, gently grasping both of her hands and smiling bravely as the men closed in to take him away.

"Thank you Miss Amber for trying to save me. Say thank you to other Treasure Rebels for me as well." He then handed her Maddox's sunglasses. "Please give these back to Mr. Maddox."

She looked at him struggling to keep her composure. Had they met a couple years sooner Darsh might have been asked by Maddox to become a member of the Treasure Rebels as well. Instead here he was, almost starved to death, his face ghost white due to blood loss, and about to be taken away and likely killed by the man who had stolen his father's identity. She had never felt sorrier for anyone in her life. He appeared the physical embodiment of defeat.

And then as he turned away she realized he had placed a key in one of her hands.

Keeping her palm closed tight she felt the steel grooves and continued to stare forward as Darsh was escorted away toward Nihar's chopper. She dared not smile.

It was an ignition key...for an airplane.

==

Minutes earlier Travis hit the water and his already bruised chest seemed to spasm for a second as most of the oxygen left his lungs. His chest felt as if he had been punched a hundred times and he immediately kicked his weightlifter-sized legs to reach the surface. But he froze as the ominous shape of the giant serpent appeared over the water's edge, and the moment he saw the repugnant glowing teeth slide into the water he spun and began swimming downwards as fast as possible.

Maddox and Amber were the finest divers in the world and due to his size and weight Travis was usually only able to swim at their top speeds in short bursts. But despite the pain in his chest he pulled himself through the water at a world record pace. He quickly reached the bottom of the strange pool fifteen feet from the surface, and with a powerful kick he launched himself in the opposite direction away from the snake curling downwards toward him.

Visibility was excellent and despite the water being ice blue in colour he was surprised to find the water was warmer than he expected. He kept kicking and entered a small passageway as the open surface above was replaced with a stone ceiling.

He kept pushing and when his chest began to tremor with lack of oxygen he didn't stop...he kicked even harder.

Suddenly the passageway ended and bright sunlight poured down from above, causing the turquoise coloured surface to shine like a million firecrackers off the stone walls. With relief he stretched both his hands upward and reached for the surface.

But then he noticed the blood.

Spinning his head he caught sight of the monstrous snake circling him from behind, leaving a trail of blackish red blood from its mutilated jaws in its wake. The grenade had torn the bottom left side of its mouth completely off, making the creature's primeval face somehow more fearsome looking than before.

The monster pulled its mangled head back...then struck.

Travis lifted his hands instinctively and grabbed onto the top and what remained of the bottom jaw as the snake lunged sluggishly forward almost enveloping his head. All Travis could do was hold on. He gritted his teeth as he pushed back on the jaws with every raw sinew and muscle in his tree trunk sized arms. The pressure on his wrists was unbearable but he didn't even feel the pain. The strength of the monstrous snake was incredible and had the serpent's mouth not been severely damaged he would never have been able to hold the jaws open for one second.

The snake corkscrewed its body but Travis's firm grip never loosened and the prehistoric teeth could not move another inch closer.

But it was still a hopeless situation for Travis. If he let go he would be chewed to pieces, but if he didn't reach the surface in moments he was going to drown...and then be eaten.

The strength in his arms was still there. But even the most powerful man can only hold his breath for so long.

Then he saw the impossible and thought.

I can't believe Yeti's can swim.

Behind the serpent and closing in fast was the twelve foot Yeti, pulling itself through the water somewhat similar in style to that of a polar bear...only much faster. The Yeti slowed down, the hideous spikes slid out of its fur covered arms, and then it kicked forward with fury only ten feet away.

Travis was certain his end had come.

Until he watched the Yeti swim behind the horrific sized snake and with a primal gurgled roar the Yeti raised both of its arms and then brought all six spikes down across the snake's meaty neck just behind the skull. Despite being underwater Travis could hear the sickening sound as the spikes sliced completely through the width of the snake's body, and he was left holding the lifeless head in his hands as the rest of the serpent's body slowly floated away.

With a bubbled grunt the Yeti seemed to howl in triumph at the kill...then with a snap of its hairy head it looked straight at Travis.

Travis immediately pushed the dead head directly towards the Yeti while he kicked his legs and shot upwards to the sunlight and safety above. But he didn't make it.

The Yeti's right clawed paw grasped his foot and began pulling him back down just as Travis's hand was only inches away from leaving the water. He couldn't hold his breath a second longer and he began to drown. He turned and prepared to kick down into the fleshy furry face as hard as he possibly could.

Then Maddox appeared.

The leader of the Treasure Rebels swam up behind the Yeti and without hesitation he wrapped both his arms around the beast's neck and began choking the creature as hard as he could. The Yeti let go of Travis and tried desperately to reach back and tear into Maddox with the claws or arm spikes. But Maddox held on and squeezed even harder as the beast's flailing arms were unable to reach him.

The second Travis was free he rocketed upwards and broke the surface. He climbed out onto the pebbles and mud coughing frantically...but finally breathing again. Wiping the water out of his eyes he was surprised to see he was at the bottom of a large hill and a shroud of fog was approaching from a large cliff face above. In the far distance the tops of the mighty Himalayas could barely be seen through the falling snow.

Below in the water Maddox waited for the right moment for the Yeti's arms to swing away from his head. Then smoothly he pulled himself up, placed both of his feet atop the beast's immense shoulders, and pushed off towards the surface.

At first the Yeti still believed Maddox was behind him. It spun and sliced through empty water. It then looked up and spotted the leader of the Treasure Rebels inches away from the surface. Opening its clawed paws it then kicked to follow.

Maddox broke the water just as the claws grasped his right leg. He submerged once again and drove his other leg squarely into the beasts' exposed throat. A weird sounding gurgle of pain emitted from the Yeti and Maddox pulled his leg free and reached again for sunlight.

But the Yeti recovered and swam up beside him, pulling its right arm back before swinging it forward in a rocking motion directly towards Maddox's chest...just as Maddox's arm pierced the surface.

Smack!

Maddox's open palm was met by Travis' outstretched hand, and with no effort Travis practically threw his friend out of the water just before the spikes would have carved into Maddox's flesh.

Maddox hit the dirt and rolled safely to a stop. Travis stumbled over and dropped onto the frosted ground beside him, still spouting small streams of blood tinged water out of his lungs and gasping for fresh oxygen.

Warily they watched for any sign of the Yeti but the water's surface remained tranquil.

"Lungs good man?"

Travis spit an enormous amount of water ten feet across the stones and smiled grimly.

"I'm good...how 'bout that shoulder?"

Maddox scratched one of the scars beneath his right eye and replied, "Better a couple hours ago."

Travis wiped his mouth and turned to reply...but stopped as the top of the Yeti's furry head finally appeared.

"Up the hill!"

Together they ran up the hundred foot incline. As they neared the top they could see Amber's red hair in the distance and the chopper's rotor blades. Panting heavily Travis quickly took a look back down. The Yeti was indeed following them up the hill, dragging something along the rocky ground as the same time.

==

Nihar's helicopter lifted off the ground pivoting southward away from the Himalayas. The con man slowly sat back in the leather co-pilot's seat and nervously sipped a small bottle of spring water.

"As fast as possible. We don't know how long we have till the police arrive."

The pilot nodded his head in acknowledgement.

Behind them in the chopper one of the mercenaries was already beginning a game of solitaire while the other was attending to Darsh, trying to set up a temporary IV bag to keep the Indian adventurer alive. Darsh despondently looked out the window as the frosted ground and the mountain peaks beyond began to shrink into the distance.

The intercom crackled to life beside Nihar's ear.

"Boss...where do I tell the men to drive the Hummer?"

Nihar replied without looking up from the Captain's logbook.

"We don't have time. Take the rest of the men in the other helicopter."

"Leave the Hummer here?"

Nihar finished the bottle and anxiously began trying to open another one.

"Torch it."

"Understood."

A couple miles below the mercenary pressed the off button on the walkie-talkie then signalled the pilot to start the take-off procedures. He then looked at the rest of Niahr's men on the hilltop.

"You all heard the boss. Get in!"

As every armed criminal began climbing inside the helo, he instead began walking towards the Hummer parked a hundred feet away. Smiling he opened the SUV's trunk and threw the keys inside. He then pulled two grenades off his belt and got ready to release the pins and hurl them inside.

Then he heard the howl.

At first he ignored it believing it came from one of the wolves far off in the distance.

But then he heard it again. It was getting closer. And it was unlike any animal he had ever heard. He looked to his right uneasily and saw Amber standing a couple hundred yards away, the other two treasure hunters running towards her...and the Yeti chasing them and drawing closer every second.

He immediately ran back towards the helicopter and leaped inside, yelling at the pilot to take off. The sliding door slammed closed and the chopper was airborne.

The Yeti reached the hilltop dragging the snake's fifty foot long body behind it, minus the head. It howled even louder as Maddox and Travis reached Amber and all three Treasure Rebels ran as one for the Hummer. But now free in the open grass the Yeti picked up even more speed and it became clear it was a hopeless attempt to reach the safety of the Hummer in time.

"We can't outrun it!"

But then the cave beast noticed the green helicopter hovering above the grass. And the thunderous roar of the rotor blades which was turning the hilltop into a blowing blizzard of frost. The beast stopped running absorbed by the sight, forgetting the Treasure Rebels completely.

Inside the helicopter the mercenaries looked out through the glass in wonder at the sight of the mythical creature. Two mercenaries quickly pulled out their smartphones to take a snapshot, but the grenade merc had a more sinister idea.

"Open the window and hand me the long range rifle."

The others quickly grinned at the idea and handed over the weapon.

He quickly pulled the trigger three times and small sprouts of dirt shot into the air at the Yeti's large feet. The beast roared and began to run in the direction of the helicopter still dragging the serpent's body, even though the chopper was now almost a hundred feet off the ground.

The Yeti stopped almost directly below the helicopter and lifted the dead snake above its head with both hairy arms. The gun happy mercenary grinned and asked the pilot to spin the chopper so he could get a clean shot.

As the pilot complied the shooter noticed the Treasure Rebels running for the Hummer for cover. He shifted the rifle and set the sight on all three of them muttering to himself, "Not so fast you celebrity creeps."

He began pulling the trigger...but was interrupted by the scream of the pilot.

He spun with the others to see the headless snake body hurtling towards the chopper, smashing directly into the cockpit glass which instantly cracked in a thousand places. The twelve hundred pound lifeless reptile body then rolled up the cockpit where it smashed into the rotor mast fracturing it in two places. The rotor blades instantly broke off spinning into the distance while the chopper corkscrewed a hundred feet downward into the cold ground...where it exploded three times and turned into a massive sizzling fireball.

Everyone on board was killed.

The blast wave shot across the hilltop just as the Rebels reached the Hummer. Using the vehicle for cover they dove onto the roof or hood and slid to safety just as pieces of debris and chunks of glass struck the Hummer's side panel and cracked the windshield. The Hummer shook as the force of the explosion briefly lifted the back wheels off the ground, causing the trunk gate to slam closed. But Maddox, Travis, and Amber were not even scratched.

Cautiously they peered around the Hummer at the destroyed chopper and the Yeti which was fearfully circling it, afraid of the flames.

"Do you think ol' Nihar will circle back?"

Amber shook her head and replied quietly to Travis.

"No, I lied to him that the police were on their way to the mansion."

Maddox lifted his healthy shoulder and tried the driver's door handle.

"Locked."

Travis quickly tried the passenger door, smacking his hand against the window in anger. It was locked as well.

Suddenly the sound of the crackling flames was replaced by that of a wolf howl. Then another cry. Then the howling from an entire pack.

The wolves had finally gotten close and slowly approached the grassy hill out of the fog, watching to see if the Yeti would yield the hill to them...and give them a chance to hunt the Treasure Rebels. Gaining confidence the three largest males bayed menacingly as a warning. But the Yeti slowly turned to face the oncoming pack and in a primal display of natural fury, the beast opened its jaws and lifting its head to the sky unleashed the loudest howl imaginable. While doing so it puffed out its body and all six spikes re-appeared out of the fur covered arms in an incredible display of hostility.

The wolves were startled at the strength behind the cry and slightly whimpering they pulled back into the fog and falling snow out of view. Within seconds the last feeble howl faded into the mountain wind. Not one wolf would ever challenge the Yeti again.

Still standing on its hind legs the Yeti silently watched the falling snow and swirling fog as it continued to roll onto the hilltop...as if it expected the wolf pack to suddenly reappear out of the mist. With the Yeti distracted the Treasure Rebels quietly moved around the Hummer to try the other doors. Finally satisfied the wolves were indeed gone, the mythical creature turned its head and stared back towards the Hummer just as the Treasure Rebels were once again in open sight.

Everyone froze.

The beast grunted but didn't move forward, its eyes half hidden beneath the fur on its face watching them closely. Maddox, Travis, and Amber stared back in awe and chilled dread. Despite hunching over slightly with pain and panting heavily in the cold air, the beast was still more powerful looking than any movie director or comic book artist could have imagined. Even the visible scars made it look more fearsome.

Still keeping their eyes focused on the Yeti, Maddox and Amber pressed their backs against the Hummer and tried the doors.

Both locked.

But Travis stood beside the trunk and slowly moved his arm until his hand grasped the latch.

Click.

It was still unlocked.

Maddox and Amber both heard the trunk open as well but no one dared move and risk encouraging the Yeti to attack.

But the Yeti didn't step forward. Instead it grunted twice...then looked squarely at Travis.

It was a strange moment. The furry face was easy for Travis to see and it was both frightening and awesome at the same time.

Then the Yeti raised both of its arms again...but this time the spikes retracted back into the hairy arms. It then barked one final grunt towards Travis. It wasn't a friendly bark like that of a dog but it wasn't a threatening howl either. It was more of a warning not to return to its territory...and almost something that resembled a farewell.

The Yeti then took two big lumbering steps and began walking slowly away towards the bottom of the hill. In seconds the beast was enveloped by the thickening fog and churning snow. One of the greatest "myths" was once again hidden from view to the outside world.

A strange stillness set in across the hilltop as the Rebels realized that for the first time in hours no predator, human or animal, was threatening them. But instead of taking a few moments to collect their thoughts they instead climbed inside the Hummer and prepared to catch Nihar.

Maddox spotted the keys and had the SUV's powerful engine roaring to life. Amber then handed the copper coloured shades to him. "Darsh found them in the cave."

He put them on hardly hearing her as he focused on adjusting the GPS. Then without looking up he handed the tablet back to her.

"Found this in the Yeti's personal swimming pool."

Grateful and stunned she quickly began testing the device to ensure it still worked.

After a couple seconds she replied, "Guys, good news, great news, and bad news."

She lifted the tablet so they could see the screen and continued, "Bad stuff first, I still can't get a signal to call the police yet, and the Hummer's phone system is linked to some sort of network owned by Nihar. If we called the cops he'd likely overhear us, but my tablet should get a signal once were out of the mountain roads. Here's the good and great stuff. Nihar took the logbook with the tracking pen still clipped to one of the pages. That means we can track his helicopter. Even better, Darsh gave me the key to his airplane he and Rhyce abandoned when they first drove up here, and he even typed the coordinates where the plane is hidden in the tablet before Nihar found him."

She read out the coordinates to Maddox who put them into the GPS after which Travis picked up the small computer and asked, "Is he still headed to the mansion?"

"According to the tracker in the pen he's taking the most direct route there."

Travis tapped the screen until Amber's pictures of the study appeared. "Think he'll take anything with him?"

"The painting. Darsh gave him a bogus story that there are clues to the treasure hidden in the old drawing."

Travis then handed Maddox the tablet who quickly began scrolling through the photos of the study. Suddenly Maddox paused and tapped the screen a few times until one of the 8k pictures was significantly magnified. He grinned and handed Amber the tablet back. Then he put the SUV in drive and crushed the accelerator.

"You both should take another look at the photos."

Puzzled she quickly began tapping the screen while Travis looked at Maddox mystified as well.

"Why?"

As the Hummer shot forward in the direction of the hidden plane, pieces of cold mud flying in all directions from the churning wheels, Maddox replied simply, "Because the Yeti Pirate's treasure is real man."

PART V: FACE TO FACE

"There's the airstrip!"

Maddox lifted his head away from the dials of the plane at the sound of Amber's voice and spotted the mansion and the expansive grounds rapidly approaching a couple miles away. Even from this distance the fading afternoon sunlight could be seen reflecting off the eight parked supercars circling the mansion's bubbling fountain.

It had been a small miracle they were able to not only find Darsh's plane quickly, but that the Indian adventurer had thankfully left behind enough reserve fuel in the containers enabling them to fly non-stop from the Himalayas directly to the mansion. Travis had even found Darsh's small revolver.

It had been a tense long flight but they had made it. They could only hope Darsh was still alive to be rescued.

"India's finest on the way."

Maddox and Amber followed Travis' gaze through the cockpit window to see ten police cars speeding along the highway a couple miles away towards the mansion estate.

"Only took them half an hour to get to it."

Amber hurriedly grabbed the tablet off the seat beside her and replied, "That's because it took hours for the tablet to get a strong enough signal, and then another hour to convince them who I was."

Maddox decreased speed and began the descent to the runway on the mansion grounds.

He adjusted the sunglasses on his face and turned to Amber.

"Tracking pen?"

Her eyes studied the data on the screen.

"Doing that now...signal good guys, hasn't moved in ten minutes. I can't exactly pinpoint location but I'd guess Nihar's still in the study."

Travis lifted a pair of high powered long distance binoculars to his eyes and studied the supercars, fountain, and front entrance as the plane continued to fly closer.

"No sign they see us comin'...large moving van parked at bottom of the steps. Nobody at the wheel...Looks like they plan to clean house before skipping town. Let's-"

He was cut off by the sound of sirens as another wave of police cars raced towards the mansion from another direction on the highway.

Nihar rapidly appeared on the marble steps, running frantically around the fountain before slamming the van doors shut and leaping into the driver's seat. Burnt rubber floated into the air as the back wheels briefly spun in protest before gripping the driveway and propelling the van out onto the road seconds before the police drove within sight of the gate.

"Tracker now moving guys...he must still have the logbook with him."

Second later the rest of Nihar's men appeared in the courtyard only to find their criminal employer had already betrayed them and left them behind. Instead of escape they now faced over a dozen guns as the police ordered them to surrender.

One of the mercenaries lifted a handgun to shoot, but a single police bullet to his tattooed arm and he was thrown backwards onto the ground near the fountain. The lawmen moved in, every mercenary put their arms into the air, and the wounded crook was lifted to his feet still breathing.

Maddox watched the van zigzag dangerously as it aggressively changed lanes and began to merge with traffic. "Mansion or van?"

"He must have left Darsh in the study!"

"Mansion it is."

After landing on the airstrip Amber had the passenger door open before the plane had come to a full stop. Travis tucked the revolver behind his back then leaped out onto the frosted tarmac to follow her towards the mansion. As fast as possible Maddox shut down the engines then ran all out to catch up, leaping up the marble steps into the mansion and ignoring the officers who barked at him to stop.

He found his friends in the study. The room was a complete mess. The Egyptian display case had been shattered and the war chariot lay on its side in the centre of the room covered in pieces of debris, broken lights, and shattered glass. Every historical item was now broken or on the floor, and the medieval desk was overturned with the supercar key stand smashed on the carpet beside it.

The stone footprint, pirate weapons, painting, uniforms, and three hooded jackets made of Yeti fur were all missing. All that remained of the Yeti Pirate artefacts was the now empty wooden frame of the cave painting, chopped to pieces and scattered across the carpeted floor.

But no sign of Darsh.

Amber lifted one of the old wooden frames now damaged beyond repair and stated irritably, "So much for Nihar's love of history."

Guns drawn the police entered the study. Amber quickly handed the lead officer her tablet and confirmed it was her who had phoned in the emergency.

The forty-something detective studied the tablet closely then turned his head and ordered the men to lower their weapons. Before he had even handed the computer back she explained, "We saw the leader of the gang drive away in a white panelled van only moments before you arrived. We last saw it heading south of here."

She then typed a quick command into the tablet and the tracking screen appeared. "See, there's the van right now! It just turned there. What is that location?" The detective studied the screen and quickly pulled a smartphone to his ear hurriedly speaking Hindi.

As they waited Maddox stepped amongst the destroyed ruins of the study. The very sight would have made a historian cry. Maddox took it all in, finally pausing at the smashed *Napoleonic Wars* display case on the floor. Everything was broken, except for one item.

On the other side of the room Travis stepped to the glass window and looked down at the courtyard below, the lights from the police cars reflecting off every supercar and the water fountain.

The detective mumbled a thank you and ended the call.

"That is a private airport. Rather small. We contacted the air traffic controller, he told us Mr. Archer has already boarded a small plane and begun preparing for take-off. We told him not to approach in case the fugitive is armed. But I am afraid we will be too late. It takes over twenty minutes to reach airport by car. But at least we have your tracker to follow his flight."

Amber responded in dread, "The tracker is limited in range. If he leaves the country we'll lose him forever...and he'll kill Darsh for certain!"

The detective replied in genuine frustration, "I am sorry, but it is basic...physics. None of our cars are fast enough to reach the airport in time. Two cars have been dispatched as we speak but they will be too late."

"What about Darsh's plane we flew here in?"

The officer swallowed in embarrassment. "When the extra squad cars arrived a few moments ago I ordered them to use the airstrip behind for parking."

"So there isn't room for the plane to take off?"

"Not until after the criminals are loaded and driven away."

Just then a small team of city police wearing jackets with the word Forensics written in Hindi entered the study carrying specialized cameras and equipment.

Relieved at the distraction the detective pointed to the door.

"This is now a crime scene and we need to have everything properly analyzed. I am sorry you three must leave. Give your statements to the officers outside. Make sure to describe Darsh Bombet so we can send out a missing person's alert immediately. We will do our best to find him."

Amber's eyes flashed in resentment but before she could argue she caught Maddox and Travis signalling her.

"We're going to do our best as well."

She then quickly followed her friends out of the study.

The forensic team immediately went to work dusting for prints and taking snapshots of everything. Thirty seconds later one of the team members lifted a plastic bag containing the sets of car keys. She called over to the detective.

"Only seven sets of keys sir. The fugitive must have taken one of the cars."

He shook his head in impatience. "No he left in a van. Besides we counted the cars. Eight were parked when we pulled in. Send all seven keys to the lab for testing. The missing set must be buried under all this mess."

"Yes sir."

But she only took three steps before the detective suddenly seized the sealed evidence bag, an alarmed look across his tired face. "Which of the car keys is missing?"

Suddenly a 16 cylinder engine roar filled the courtyard.

"The Bugatti Chiron."

===

(Fifteen Minutes Later)

"Runway not clear for take-off. Runway under repairs. I repeat *not* clear for take-off."

Nihar slowly sat back in the leather pilot's seat, ignored the flight controller and increased the engine power. The bluish white small private jet rumbled with noise and the wheels accelerated. He was going to use this old abandoned and dirt covered runway, and no-one could stop him in time.

Nihar's small lips curled into an odd smile beneath the tangled hair of his goatee...the smug smile of a man who knows he's escaping justice. He looked back at the small cargo compartment where the footprint, painting canvas, and pirate artefacts were securely stored. He then looked down at the pirate logbook on the co-pilot's seat, Amber's special pen still attached to the ancient pages.

He knew a couple thieves in Australia who owed him a favour or two, the kind of men who would extract every secret in the Captain's old book and the oil painting once given the chance. He would call them to set up a meeting in Sydney in the next few days.

"Please respond and shut down engines."

Nihar simply laughed. The fool in the control tower was wasting his breath.

"There's a car on the runway. Repeat a car on the runway."

Nihar suddenly had to respond.

"*What* on the runway?"

"A black and dark purple car. Extremely fast and coming up on your tail. Cancel take-off immediately."

Nihar tossed the headphones in a panicked frenzy and increased the power even more. In a few seconds he would be airborne.

That's when the multi-million super sports car shot into view along the runway a safe distance to his left. The speed of the car was incredible, and the Chiron left behind in its wake a wild swirling cloud of dust. Even up in the plane's cabin Nihar could hear the thunderous engine as the car accelerated even more. Soon all he could see was the red LED taillight in the churning dirt cloud ahead.

The red taillight suddenly flashed bright red as the driver hit the brakes and the multimillion dollar car began to slow down...directly in the plane's path.

Nihar anxiously looked down at the dials and tried to lift the plane as the black spoiler of the Chiron began to edge closer and closer. This was his last chance. But the wheels remained stuck to the dirty tarmac. He simply didn't have enough power yet to leave gravity behind.

In an act of survival he cancelled the take-off to avoid a major collision. After thirty long seconds the small jet engine aircraft slowly rolled to a stop while the Chiron smoothly turned so the super sports car was now parallel with the airstairs which were gradually descending to the ground.

Nihar hurriedly lifted a suitcase from beneath the passenger seat. A suitcase filled with rupees.

Nihar knew it had to be the Bugatti from the mansion. The one he chose to drive to make a powerful impression when trying to con others. The only question was who was behind the wheel now. Only a handful of drivers would have had the skill and guts to pull off such a dangerous move to stop the plane from taking off. Nihar guessed it was one of his men from the mansion who had escaped and would be demanding he take him out of the country as well. Or more likely a young officer looking for promotion had jumped into one of the cars and followed him to the airport looking to make a career changing big arrest.

He lifted the hefty suitcase and began scampering down the steps hoping the officer would care more for money than any promotion.

But he stumbled and dropped the case in stunned surprise, which clattered down the steps until it smashed onto the runway and burst open, rupees flying into the air in every direction.

Waiting for him at the bottom were the Treasure Rebels. Travis and Amber each stood calmly against the car's side panel while Maddox instead sat atop the luxury car, his sunglasses almost blinding Nihar as they reflected the sunlight. The longest second in Nihar's life passed as the conman stared at the three treasure hunters. Then his eyes caught the reflection of police lights in the distance reflecting off the Chiron's black and purple paint. Instantly he bolted back up the stairs.

Click.

He slowly turned to see Travis holding Darsh's small revolver, the safety now pulled back.

"Where's Darsh?"

The conman slowly stepped onto the ground and pointed up at the plane. "In the main cabin."

Amber swiftly climbed the steps. Once inside she began tossing the artefacts aside until she found Darsh propped up against the cabin wall, unconscious and barely breathing. She hurriedly leaned her head outside and signalled the others below that Darsh was indeed in the plane. She then disappeared back inside to stabilize Darsh as best she could until the medics arrived.

Down by the Bugatti Travis walked up to Nihar and stared face to face with the man who had nearly gotten him and his friends killed.

Nihar stared back defiantly...but his eyes betrayed the anguish he felt. The con man's mask had finally been ripped away and all that was left was the weak criminal who had no tricks left to try. He had lived in luxury in another man's home pretending to be a kind hearted philanthropist, now he would share a sparse jail cell for the rest of his life with cold blooded felons like himself.

Travis finally spoke as the police cars skidded to a stop around the plane.

"It's a good thing you asked us to rescue Darsh...we just didn't realize he needed rescuing from you."

He then stepped to the side as Maddox jumped off the Chiron and walked up.

Nihar kept his temper in check with Travis but couldn't help snarling in resentment at the sight of Maddox. For the first time in years the world heard Nihar's true voice, a mixture of Indonesian and New Zealand accents combined as one.

"We finally get to meet. The famous Maddox Tarver. Famous only because you've found a little treasure in the ocean and yet without me you would now be a corpse in that awful jungle. The newspapers, the websites, they turned you into a celebrity. But the real life Maddox Tarver is...a sad disappointment."

Maddox completely ignored the meaningless insults and just grinned, "Thanks for finding me when you did man. Because if you hadn't I would never have gotten the chance to meet you in person to do this." Triumphantly he placed the Napoleonic era handcuffs he had taken from the study onto Nihar's wrists, closing them shut with a loud cracking snap.

As he did so the police stepped in and escorted Nihar away to one of the patrol cars. Meanwhile the medics rushed up the steel steps at Travis' direction and began to assist Darsh.

The same detective from the mansion hurriedly stepped forward and tapped Travis on the shoulder while pointing at the black revolver. Travis quickly handed it over as the detective asked guardedly, "You weren't planning on some sort of execution out here were you?"

"It was just for self defense...and for show."

The officer looked at Travis then at the gun puzzled, "Just for show?"

He then felt the weight of the gun and opened it to look at the bullet chambers. It was empty.

Together he and Travis both laughed. "Just for show indeed!"

Maddox watched as Darsh was carried carefully down the steps tied to a stretcher, Amber climbing down behind the procession smiling brightly. The young treasure hunter from India was going to make it.

The leader of the Treasure Rebels then turned back to Travis as the detective placed the gun into an evidence bag. "I didn't know the gun was a dummy."

Travis smiled, "Stupid Nihar didn't know it either."

But the conman wasn't completely finished. He twisted in anger tossing one of the officers to the ground just for the chance to yell one last insult.

"The Treasure Rebels are just a fraud! You will never find the Yeti Pirate's treasure!" As the police roughly seized him and pushed him towards the car, the conman pointed his head towards Darsh as the stretcher was being loaded into the ambulance.

"And that weak piece of trash...everything he did will be for nothing!"

Nihar hoped to hear a response but before anything could be said he was tossed into the backseat and the bullet proof door was slammed shut in his face.

Seconds later the ambulance doors were closed and the driver took off, leaving behind actual skid marks on the tarmac.

Amber watched until the lights and sirens had faded into the distance. Walking back over to her friends she stared angrily at Nihar who sat quietly in the police car, his face and shoulders shrouded in darkness by the tinted glass.

Seeing all three of the Treasure Rebels finally together the detective walked over to shake their hands. "Thank you for your help in apprehending Nihar Archer. He is wanted by Interpol and there may be reward for you three for helping to catch him. But I need you to come with me to the station for a full report...and for a full good meal as well."

The police car carrying Nihar pulled away and the detective continued, "I hope your friend in the ambulance did not hear that rather cruel insult from Mr. Archer. After the injuries he sustained he will not be looking for treasure anytime soon."

They just laughed.

"We hope he did!"

When he saw their triumphant smiles he replied incredulously, "You do not know where this treasure is...do you?

Travis just pointed at Maddox. "He already figured it out."

"Where Mr. Tarver?"

Sitting atop the Chiron Maddox smiled confidently and pointed at the now quiet plane.

"Right here on the tarmac with us!"

EPILOGUE: PIRATE SOUVENIRS

(One Week Later – New Delhi Hospital)

The old taxi slowed to a stop outside the main hospital doors. The three passengers hurriedly paid the elderly driver who smiled at his good fortune as they placed a large stack of rupees into his shaking hand for a ten minute drive through the afternoon traffic.

Maddox, Travis, and Amber stepped through the revolving glass doors and nodded to the security guard who waved them through. Ignoring the stares from the rest of the hospital staff they entered the sleek elevator just before the stainless steel doors closed. In thirty seconds the digital light blinked and a dull beep echoed from the speaker in the ceiling to signal they had reached the top floor. The doors smoothly clicked open and they walked out into the recovery ward. Moments later Amber knocked on the last door at the end of the hall, where a nurse inside called out that they could enter.

The room was small but inviting and a large window gave the only patient an incredible view of downtown New Delhi while allowing warm sunlight to pour inside. Darsh smiled as the Treasure Rebels entered. He still looked painfully thin and his chest was bandaged from multiple broken ribs and two surgeries. But his strength was back and his eyes were once again sharp and full of energy.

"I'm going to live!"

They laughed and cheered along with him. Maddox and Travis each shook his hand in congratulations while Amber hugged him. It was the first time they had seen him since the rescue at the airport.

Beside the bed the nurse calmly smiled, while still failing to hide her puzzled expression at seeing what the Rebels were wearing.

"I will be back with the doctor in about twenty minutes."

As she left Amber handed the leather logbook to Darsh. "Nihar left it on the plane. It certainly belongs to you."

He gratefully took it and stared at the olden pages lost in thought. Suddenly the joy was gone in his eyes and a quiet sadness filled the room.

"I did hear Nihar yell at me when I was being taken to the ambulance. He's right, everything I did led to nothing. There was no gold in the Yeti cave, and whatever treasure the pirates stored away from their years of sailing will probably never be found. All I did was blindly trust bad people, nearly get myself killed, and have a monster like that Nihar almost steal my father's name."

He looked out at the city through the window and continued, "The police told me that some items from my home have gone missing. Nihar and his men must have sold them off weeks before." A faint smile returned to his face.

"It is actually okay. The most important family items have been recovered, and Nihar's attempted destruction of my family's historical artefacts, like the war chariot, along with my testimony, will increase his long prison sentence! I look forward to giving my testimony against him and every one of his associates."

Travis grinned, "We all left lengthy statements with the cops, that'll help the prosecutors even more."

"Thank you. And thank you for saving me. I never met or spoke with you Treasure Rebels until that day we met in the pirate cave, and yet you three did more for me than anyone else has since my father died."

"We're glad we could help. But to be honest man, Nihar also tricked the three of us into coming here to India."

Darsh closed the old book and placed it onto the table beside his bed, unconcerned at Maddox's admission.

"That is okay, I know about Nihar's finding you in the Amazon."

A brief moment passed until Darsh followed up with the obvious question.

"Why are you all wearing the Yeti hoodies?"

Instead of a direct answer Maddox replied, "We're actually glad you heard Nihar taunt you about never finding treasure!"

"You're *glad*?"

Without a response Maddox took off his hoodie and snapped open a serrated titanium scuba diver's knife and cut across the bottom seam of the ancient fur jacket.

Darsh watched horrified until Maddox lifted the hoodie over his head...where a hundred gold coins spilled out onto the bed, some clattering onto the floor while the rest remained at Darsh's feet, a small mountain of pirate treasure!

Amber and Travis immediately did the same to the hoodies they were wearing as well, until Darsh and his entire bed was covered in three hundred gold coins.

"The pirates sowed the gold into their hoodies to get past the port authorities."

Darsh threw some of the coins into the air laughing, "How did you know?"

Maddox pointed at Amber's tablet velcroed to her arm. "Nihar took Amber and Travis through the mansion and showed them the Yeti Pirate artefacts. She took pictures of the pirate display and when I got to look at them I noticed one of the coins sticking out of the bottom lining in the fur. It was obvious to me the pirates had hidden the coins inside the hoodies to sneak past the port authorities, the remaining gold from their days attacking ships in the Indian Ocean. After more than two hundred years the lining was finally beginning to tear away to reveal the treasure inside."

"But how did you spot it, and not me or Nihar? I found these hoodies over half a year ago and Nihar would have had a month to study them as well!"

Amber replied, "My tablet takes photos in 8k quality. What Maddox saw was a magnification no human eye could see on its own. Only one twentieth of an inch of the coin was sticking out of the fabric. Nihar would have had to open the case and literally put the coat under a microscope to spot it."

Travis explained further, "All the rest of your Yeti Pirate stuff is back at the mansion including the oil painting. All of it will be considered priceless now."

"You three deserve a cut in the treasure too! Take as many coins as you want!"

Maddox shook his head and laid the pirate jacket onto the bottom of the bed.

"No man, you found all the artefacts, the treasure and glory belongs to you."

Darsh then noticed for the first time that all three Rebels were covered in small cuts and bruises, and that Maddox was wearing a brand new sling to support his injured shoulder.

Meanwhile Travis' broken left hand was tightly wrapped in bandages from the Yeti fight.

"But look what you all went through. You deserve something!"

He then grabbed his smartphone off the table and began sending a text message.

"I already gave this some thought, you are going to get a good reward for all you did to rescue me."

Before anyone could refuse he continued, "The authorities have sealed off the cave and will decide what to do next. As of right now the scientists are debating what the right course of action will be. Some believe an expedition should return to capture the snakes, others think it is too deadly and the cave system should be sealed off permanently."

He tapped send on the screen and looked up, "But the scientists and media still do not know about the Yeti."

"They're going to realize he's real when they see the treasure."

Darsh's phone pinged and he quickly read the reply text before answering Travis.

"All of Nihar's men who saw the creature died in the helicopter explosion. So only us four actually saw the Yeti. I do not know whether to tell the scientists or not. If I do, the entire world will swarm over the Himalayas looking for him, and more lives will likely be lost. I think it's better the Yeti is left alone. Unless I can think of a good reason he should be found."

He then lifted the hoodie lined with Yeti fur and handed it back to Maddox.

"It is best then these be kept out of sight...you three keep them as souvenirs!"

Maddox humbly took the fur jacket once worn by a pirate and put it back on.

"Gnarly."

Just then the door opened and a middle-aged Indian man dressed in a dark blue suit and carrying a black leather briefcase walked purposefully into the room. Behind him an Indian women in her mid-twenties wearing a blue dress followed behind. She waved at everyone then blew Darsh a kiss before quietly waiting near the door. Clearly Darsh's girlfriend.

The man politely nodded to the Treasure Rebels then spoke directly to Darsh, seemingly ignoring the hundreds of pirate coins scattered across the tiled floor and piled atop the bed.

"I received the text sir. Paperwork is ready for the signatures."

"Terrific! Now look outside the window Treasure Rebels. Look down at the street!"

They followed Darsh's instruction, unbelieving at what they saw sitting below the window.

The eight supercars from the mansion.

"My lawyer here has prepared the documents for ownership transfer. Each of you can choose whatever car you wish! I have arranged transport with a large cargo plane so all three cars will be sent home safely with you to the United States."

Amber turned away from the window. "No, it just isn't right Darsh. These hoodies are more than enough reward. We would feel awkward-"

"Please take one at least! I would feel very insulted otherwise!"

When Maddox and Travis also politely declined, Darsh jumped out of bed spilling coins everywhere before hobbling over to Travis.

"I saw you fight the Yeti. Your bravery is why we are all still here! Your...your...decision to fight the creature by yourself, it is something that I cannot ignore and must reward."

"Just another fight I'm-"

"No...please take the car you really want to drive."

Travis hesitated then looked back out the window. It somehow seemed wrong now to say no.

Off to the side the lawyer noticed Travis hesitate. Swiftly he clicked open a pen ready to write. "Where's home for you three?"

Amber pulled the hoodie around her face and looked outside at the skyline in the distance.

"Miami."

==

(Four Days Later – Miami)

The beautiful black and dark purple Chiron pulled out of Miami International Airport and quietly merged into traffic. With a quick tap of the gas pedal the engine gave a momentary roar as the supercar briefly accelerated down an open stretch of road, headed towards the condos and apartments lining the beach.

"This is wild!"

"You liked it the moment Nihar drove it onto that beach in Brazil trying to impress us."

She then looked out at the Miami skyscrapers in the distance while enjoying the warm breeze through the open window. She hadn't been home in a long time and had forgotten how much she missed Florida's biggest city.

Suddenly her tablet began ringing

"Hi Dad!"

"Are you three back in Miami yet?"

"We landed twenty minutes ago and are headed to you right now."

"Excellent! Everyone feeling well after your adventure in India? I caught the news, they weren't very detailed as usual...but I spotted Maddox wearing that sling in the background."

She looked at the side view mirror where Maddox could be seen a hundred feet back effortlessly riding his Triumph Street Scrambler motorcycle.

"I wouldn't worry about the arm, the sling's gone and he's able to ride his favourite bike again better than ever."

"Very good. But I thought he would want to ride in that special car you told me about?"

She stretched her legs and replied, "There's only two seats and despite the excellent room in here Maddox and I could barely fit inside when Travis drove to the airport to stop the conman. He's more than happy driving his Scrambler."

Back at the Treasure Rebels "headquarters" near the Miami beaches, sixty year old Dr. Gunnar Monette nodded his head but barely listened to her reply. Instead he walked across the large office space his daughter and friends had set up for him. With his almost bald head, lab coat, and gaunt six foot tall build he looked little different than hundreds of other scientists around the globe. But there was nothing ordinary about his incredible achievements over the last twenty years as a world leading mathematician, physicist, and biologist.

In the centre of the well lit room was a long rectangle table where the artefacts and other treasured items the Rebel's had found in Egypt, Congo, and the Amazon were placed. Wolfgang's journal, the recovered safe and vials of medicine, the strange flag and treasured dive helmet, and every picture from the tablet and goggle cameras...it was all there.

Dr. Gunnar stopped in front of the safe and pulled out a small pile of papers from within.

"Did you know that Nazi fiend Wolfgang was an artist?"

Amber grimaced, "Yes, I've seen his sketches of wildlife in his journal."

"No I mean the ones of astronomy."

"Astronomy?"

"Yes, stored in the safe you three recovered in the Congo are dozens of sketches he made of outer space."

"Not aliens please."

He laughed. "Of course not, but of stars, meteor showers, and a rather detailed drawing of Saturn. Is that helpful for your search?"

"Probably not. You left a message about the flag from the Amazon?"

"Oh yes!"

He walked to the end of the table and lifted the worn military flag under a high powered lamp.

"I took samples of the flag and the blood drops on it are about 1,700 years old."

"What! Can you even estimate what battle it was sent into?"

"Even better my daughter. I can identify the group of soldiers who used the flag...or something like soldiers."

Amber sat up excitedly, "This is terrific Dad! How did you do it?"

He placed the flag carefully back into the plastic container and walked to the end of the table. There resting on a metal platform was the golden diver helmet covered in jewels and white diamonds.

"The key was no database, it was the helmet. It's not real."

"Not real? Dad we-"

"No no! I meant it's made of real parts but...it's not a real diving helmet."

"Dad, I can't-"

"I was able to pull it apart."

She nearly dropped the tablet.

He chuckled for a second when he realized how he sounded.

"Don't worry! I discovered a release mechanism within the metal frame. The whole scuba helmet is really some sort of container."

"So the gold and jewels are cheap imitations?"

"The jewels, the diamonds, the gold, it is all authentic. It's just an even greater treasure is hidden inside."

Amber paused and looked mystified at Travis who had been listening along as well.

"What kind of treasure Dad?"

Dr. Monette put the smartphone onto the table then with a grunt lifted the heavy antique helmet.

"I'm opening it again so I can better describe it to you."

He grasped the face plate and turned it to the right. A dull click followed. He then pulled the plate back to its former spot, then to the right again.

The helmet split in two pieces, revealing a smaller *military* helmet inside...worn in combat almost two millennia ago.

"It is a gladiator helmet from the Roman Empire. It's made of bronze and is in almost perfect condition except for three small pieces which are missing out of the face guard. It clearly saw combat in some arena or battlefield. There are even Roman drawings on the top of the helmet which tell a story you three will not believe!"

"Dad you are brilliant!"

"I understand that the Rainforest Rogue left the dive helmet in the jungle decades ago?"

"That's right, Maddox was the first to find it since then."

Dr. Monette put the gladiator helmet down and sighed unhappily.

"A little sad the Rainforest Rogue did not live long enough to see what was hidden inside."

He then looked at every exotic treasure and item scattered across the long table his expression now serious.

"There are different clues to study, but I believe they all point to a specific location where you and your swashbuckling friends will finally find what you've been looking for these past couple years."

"Maddox will be thrilled! Where are we heading?"

"Scuba diving the Mediterranean."

"Wonderful! No more caves or jungles, just back to the beautiful blue ocean!"

She typed on the screen and a map of the world's oceans appeared. She then tapped the image of the Mediterranean Sea until every port and known shipwreck site was displayed.

"Okay, do you have a good estimation of where we need to dive?"

Dr. Monette looked up at a whiteboard on the opposite wall covered in blue and green scribbles that only a genius would understand. "A general estimation, but more than workable for you and your friends." He then read off a series of coordinates.

When he didn't hear a reply he continued, "Are you still there? Did you get all of those headings?"

She finally replied but her voice had suddenly lost its enthusiasm.

"I got them...are you sure that's the area? The infamous one where all the sharks are?"

"I am certain."

He picked up the phone, surprised at her obvious unease.

"This isn't like you to be afraid of a dive. Even one with sharks. What is wrong?"

She turned to Travis who shook his head, just as concerned as she was.

With a heavy heart she finally replied, "It's the very spot Maddox was attacked by the blue shark...what gave him all the scars."

She then looked back at Maddox, his copper shades brightly reflecting the burning Miami sunlight in the mirror's reflection.

"It's the only place he promised never to dive again."

Don't miss out!

Visit the website below and you can sign up to receive emails whenever Gerard Doris publishes a new book. There's no charge and no obligation.

https://books2read.com/r/B-A-WRCD-IGOY

BOOKS 2 READ

Connecting independent readers to independent writers.

Did you love *India Yeti Pirates*? Then you should read *Greek Gladiator Sharks*[1] by Gerard Doris!

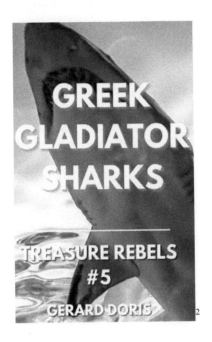

Every dive. Every enemy. Every perilous wild adventure.

The Treasure Rebels have survived it all to get to this point. Now one step away from the treasure they have been searching for years to find, the world's greatest treasure hunters must dive the most treacherous shark infested stretch of water in the world to finally complete their crucial mission.

Scuba diving in the Aegean Sea amongst isolated Greek islands, the Rebels must explore the exotic underwater ruins of an ancient gladiator school. But as they embark on their most important dive ever, Maddox, Travis, and Amber are unaware the greatest danger may be waiting for them above the waves.

"Greek Gladiator Sharks" is the fifth adventure in the Treasure Rebels novella series, and directly follows the astonishing events of "India Yeti Pirates."

Read more at https://www.adventurefictionforever.com.

Also by Gerard Doris

Treasure Rebels
Nile River Scorpion
Congo Spider Fangs
Amazon Swamp Victory
India Yeti Pirates
Greek Gladiator Sharks

Standalone
Wrath of the Renegades

Watch for more at https://www.adventurefictionforever.com.

About the Author

Thanks for reading! I write adventure fiction that features treasure hunters, pirates, and renegades. I'm also a fan of NFL football, westerns, classic action movies, and anything that promotes genuine adventure. For some fun updates on my writing projects, you can follow me on Twitter at https://twitter.com/gerard_advfict

Read more at https://www.adventurefictionforever.com.

Milton Keynes UK
Ingram Content Group UK Ltd.
UKHW040947071123
432124UK00001B/24

9 798223 228349